SLEEPING HELENA

Other Books by Erzebet YellowBoy

The Bone Whistle (as Eva Swan)
Grandmother's House (forthcoming)
The Land of Dreams (forthcoming)

SLEEPING HELENA

Erzebet YellowBoy

PRIME BOOKS

SLEEPING HELENA

Prime Books
www.prime-books.com

For more information, contact Prime Books.

ISBN: 978-1-60701-212-2

for Dis & Dubh

CHAPTER 1

KITTY WAS A TALL WOMAN, WIDE AT THE SHOULDER AND heavy of thigh, who kept her white braids coiled on top of her head, held in place by an army of hairpins. Her skin was a deep shade of sepia and she wore lipstick the color of those halfling cherries found lurking at the bottom of canned fruit cup. She was sometimes forgiving and sometimes not. On the day of her grandniece's christening she was not, and she knew just who to blame for the grave insult.

The eldest of eight sisters, Kitty had been born blind. At the age of five she'd fallen from a horse and into a coma that had lasted for seven long days. When she woke, Kitty could *See*. The visions that revealed the future to her were dreadful episodes, but none were as awful as she became as the years passed by. Kitty's sisters often wished she'd never woken from her coma at all. Even so, none ever slighted her as they had done now.

Kitty did not need an invitation to the christening, of course, but it still would have been nice to get one. It would have been *right* to get one. She was one of child's grandaunts, was she not?

Poor Lena, Kitty thought, and then, *It is better this way*.

ജ രു

Lena, orphaned daughter of a distant cousin, had been taken in by Kitty's sisters and raised as though she was their own. They had intended to send her to university; it would have been a fine thing to help her pack her bags and dress her in the pretty green suit and matching hat they had purchased for the occasion. They were so looking forward to shipping her off, proudly and in state, to start her new life. Instead Lena had fallen for the charms of an errant boy. He had planted his seed in her as though she'd been his own private garden and then left her for the sisters to tend.

Although disappointed, Kitty's sisters had swarmed around Lena and her disgraceful belly like bees around a hive. When Lena had died giving birth to her daughter, the sisters had done the only thing they could. They named the baby Helena, for her mother, and decided to keep her as well.

The christening, the sisters hoped, would help ease the pain of their recent loss. The house was full of chattering guests and the tables were laden with food. Streamers hung from the ceiling and the curtains were strewn with tiny, sparkling white lights. The sisters had put a great deal of effort into this joyful event.

By the time Kitty arrived the priest was gone, summarily dismissed by the horde of elderly women surrounding Helena, the baby in her cradle almost lost amidst their bulk. They crowded about like hovering zeppelins, ever too high to reach.

The grandaunts shuffled and clucked until finally Thekla, second eldest of the eight sisters, called the women to attention.

Thekla was tall and her knees were great knobs below a skirt the others felt her wardrobe would be better off without. They whispered to each other about days gone by, when a dress was the proper length for a lady and such knees were never seen. Thekla clapped her hands for silence.

"Sisters!" she shouted. "And others," she added as an afterthought, for there was surely a great host in attendance. Relations and friends had come from all corners to witness Helena's christening.

"It is time to bestow the gifts upon the babe Helena. Gather round, will you, and no shoving." She glared at Ingeburg, a wobbly sister some seven years younger than herself. She had bumbled directly into Thekla and gotten her skirt twisted around her cane when she tried to edge away.

The crowd pressed in and their eyes grew wide in eager anticipation. The power to give exceptional gifts was the sisters' inheritance, passed down through their mother's line through time immemorial. No shirts and ties, or ugly clocks, or trinkets from afar would Helena receive—the gifts her aunts would give were of a different sort, more ephemeral and far more lasting. It was a delicate business; the family had learned through trial, error, and pure foolishness that some things were better off not given. The sisters had agreed well beforehand on what each would give to Helena.

The grandest aunts a child ever had surrounded the cradle in which Helena belched in happy ignorance of their intent. In order of age they stood, oldest to youngest: Thekla, the twins Helga and Hilda, Zilli, Ingeburg, Eva, and Elfrieda. Seven sisters in all crowded round with joy, heaving and sweating and stinking of powder and fumes. The remainder of the family—other aunts, uncles, cousins—all shuffled behind them, peering and prying as best as they could to get a glimpse of the tiny child.

Dark as a storm cloud and bearing the threat of lightning, Kitty strode into the throng of skirts and buns that cooed and gurgled like babes themselves around the infant girl. Helena, a fresh one-month-old, was unimpressed by their noises and content to spill her drool down her small, pink chin. As the masses parted, her tiny eyes landed on the woman who had driven them away.

What Helena saw then is known only to her, for who really knows how small ones see the world and those within it? She may have been attracted to the cherry lips, or to the snowy mound of hair rising over the powdered creases and valleys of Kitty's skin. All that can be told for certain is that Helena's greening eyes met the pale blues of Aunt Kitty, and her drooling and her burping ceased along with all of the murmurs and hiccups of the well-watered klatsch.

"What a pretty girl she is," Kitty said as she stood over the babe. "Yes," Kitty bent her great self so that her own nose nearly met the tiny bud of Helena's, "you are quite the young lady."

The huddle of women drew in their breaths as Kitty straightened and turned her eyes upon them. "Have you given the gifts without me?" she asked the crowd.

Dear god, I should have invited her. Thekla paled, but quickly gathered her wits. "No. We have not."

"Do begin! Do not let my presence stop you." Kitty's bright lips cracked in a friendly smile.

Thekla rearranged her skirt and gestured sharply for El-frieda, the youngest of the sisters. Elfrieda's visage had graced the silver screen in the days of silent pictures, much to the dismay of her more conservative sisters. Even at her advanced age, she retained the softness and clear skin that reveals how glorious her face must have been in youth. Elfrieda valued beauty and surrounded herself with only the most beautiful things. Her gift was that Helena should become beautiful, so she might use beauty to pave an easier way through life if she so chose.

Gifts were historically granted in order, from the youngest to the oldest, but Eva, next in line, had seemingly vanished. Thekla saw Kitty smile and flinched, but she would not be daunted. She called Ingeburg to the babe's side.

Ingeburg was admired for her great intelligence. Educated in the finest universities, she had gathered other illuminati about her for most of her life. Many were the scholars to dine at her table, partaking of her conversation and philosophy. Her gift to Helena was a superior intellect, so she could outsmart all who might stand in the way of her success.

Zilli followed Ingeburg. If it were not for her wrinkles and the wisps of grey hair, one might think she was not so old. Her graceful form bent over Helena, who shrieked and raised a tiny fist at her lovely aunt. Zilli, who charmed all with ease, passed her gift of grace to the child, so she could melt every heart that might otherwise wish her ill.

The twins Helga and Hilda approached as a pair, their long legs swinging with matched motion, like an ancient clockwork toy. Helga's voice had been like birdsong echoing over the lake in the morning. Hilda's movements had been the sway of a willow on the lakeshore by night. They had performed as one to great acclaim and they knew the worth of themselves. They united their gifts in Helena: song and dance, so her voice would be sweet and her limbs supple enough to surpass her twin aunts, if she pleased.

Thekla moved forward once they were finished. Thekla, before her hands were put to other uses, was a pianist of wondrous talent, destined for fame. She gave Helena music, so that from any instrument she could draw such sound as to sear an unwary soul. Thekla balled her own hands into fists. Music was no longer theirs to beckon; she had stopped playing years ago.

Thekla's eyes narrowed as Kitty approached and smiled down at the babe. A shiver ran through Thekla. Her sister smelled of the forest, and the shadow she cast was as black as those in its depths.

There was nothing Thekla could do about Kitty's intentions. Kitty was the oldest and due a turn and in their family, dues were always paid.

"I *See* many things ahead of you," Kitty said to Helena and then laughed as Helena belched in response.

"You will grow well and tall, like the trees in that black wood from which your ancestors spread forth, and you will thrive on the gifts you've been given. But you will not always be content, my child," she said as she leaned down to whisper in Helena's crisp, pink ear. In the breathless silence, everyone heard her all too well. "The window of time will break all around you; you'll want to prick your own finger on its keenest edge."

The crowd sighed. Kitty raised her head as though the

ceiling spoke. Her eyes became white crescents in her face. Thekla put a hand to her mouth in fear.

They all watched as Kitty's eyes slowly cleared and focused on the child. They were all stunned by the words that fell from her cruelly painted mouth.

Death shall lead you back
in time and place
to that unwitting day,
when all was lost
at too dear a cost
in the water's cold embrace.

She blinked and the gift was given.

The crowd shuddered and gasped, their bulk rolling to and fro as they gathered themselves and shoved about, all wanting to reach Helena and flee Kitty's words at the same time. Kitty, who had no more to say to anyone, gave Helena a dainty kiss on her cheek and departed while her sisters tried to recover what senses remained. Helena was left in a sea of confusion, a small thing, unknowing and unaware.

CHAPTER 2

"WAIT."

Faces turned as Eva stepped out of the crowd.

"There is still one gift to give."

The words silenced them. Thekla tensed as all eyes settled on her sister.

"Be assured," Eva said, "that though I cannot take back what our wild sister has given, I can soften Kitty's words. I give the gift of sleep instead of death."

The matrons and maids and aunts and uncles sighed. It seemed little better, but it would have to do and they eagerly dissipated soon after. The ballroom, full of laughter and chatter and plates overflowing just an hour ago, now held the remains of the feast and a few forgotten stoles in its wide, empty space.

Hope, the sisters' housekeeper turned nursemaid, bent over Helena's cradle and scooped her up. As she carried the fussing baby off to bed, Hope whispered a promise of her own into Helena's ear.

"Don't worry, little one. Whatever happens," she said to Helena, "I will do my best mend it."

The sisters never heard her. Their canes tapped the floor

and china clattered as they rearranged abandoned plates on the crumb-scattered table. The sound of it ground Thekla's nerves into dust. She would have to stay up all night writing letters of apology for the sad ending to what should have been a day of joy.

Thekla gathered her sisters in the drawing room when they were finished. Under ordinary circumstances, it was a cozy room. In winter a fire blazed brightly in a hearth that was now clean and cold. A waning sun shed pallid light through lead-paned windows. On a softly illumined wall hung a painting of their brother, wrought by an artist who attained a brief pinnacle of fame well after his own demise. This evening the room seemed too small and Thekla imagined a goblin at every window peering in to laugh at the grand failure of the day.

She glanced at the painting, dulled slightly with time. Their brother Louis stood in front of a different fireplace, much grander than any the sisters now knew, with his hand balled smartly on his hip. He was young, no more than sixteen years old, but Thekla could see the man he would have become. His hair formed a halo of black curls around his head and he was smiling. His eyes in the painting shone, though their light was a product of the artist's fancy. Louis' eyes had always been dark as night. He peered out at them from a world much different than their own. Thekla wondered, not for the first time, how things might have been had he lived to an old age with the rest of them.

Zilli spoke first. "What in all of creation brought Katza here and in such a fury, and what do you suppose she meant by all of that?"

Despite the frowns, coughs and pointed glances of her sisters' objections, Zilli used Kitty's proper, given name. The others had begun to refer to Katza as *Kitty* after their move to America. They did not want to associate their homeland with the sister who had stayed there. Zilli, though, simply preferred the sound of their mother tongue.

Thekla sniffed. "She intends for the child to die. You all heard her. She's as cruel as ever—as I've always warned you she would be."

"Surely we've given her no reason to despise the child so. Why would she wish her ill?" Eva saw Thekla turn away. "She was invited to the christening, wasn't she?"

The sisters looked to each other, nodded slowly, uncertainly, until the last of their eyes fell on Thekla, who drew in her breath.

"Kitty did not receive an invitation. I was unaware that she even knew of Helena's existence. It is nothing but spite that drove her to darken our door today." Thekla was seething and her face was flushed was anger. A stranger would have wondered that her withered frame could support such feeling, but her sisters knew that in truth, the feeling supported the frame.

"Thekla," Ingeburg could not believe her sister had been so foolish, "you know perfectly well our sister knew about the christening."

Eyes lowered. Kitty *Saw* everything. Of course she had known. No one else would say it, however. Thekla knew best where Kitty was concerned. After all, she was the only one who truly remembered their eldest sister.

"What is done, is done," Eva said into the silence. "You are right, Zilli, to question what Kitty meant as opposed to her reasons for doing it. We may never know what moves our sister, but even she would not take such offense over such a slight as to give death to an innocent child."

"You don't know her. Not as I do," Thekla said.

The sisters shifted in their seats, relaxed. None wanted to challenge Thekla, especially on this night.

"*Death shall lead you back*, she said," offered Ingeburg. "I don't suppose any of you comprehend that phrase any better than I?" Ingeburg felt that she, of all the sisters, should have a ready answer to the riddle. That she did not was cause for amazement; for the first time in Ingeburg's life she judged her mind lacking.

"*Back* to what, is what I would like to know," said Eva. "I do wish I could have also countered that, but as you all know, such is not in my power."

"We don't blame you, dear. Saving your gift till last was a thrice-worthy act. More than we might have hoped for." Thekla, ashamed she did not think of it herself, shook her head.

Elfrieda, strangely silent during the discourse, looked Thekla in the eye. "You know what she wants," she said with a firm voice that shocked her sisters into silence. "You know what fancies burn her. You recall the letters, do you not?"

A murmuring came to life in the room as the sisters spoke softly to themselves and to each other. Ingeburg was astounded by her most vapid sister's declaration. Suddenly it all made terrible sense. The twins said nothing, but slouched a little further down into their seats. Zilli's mouth hung open and Thekla bit her lip. They were old. Most of them had *not*, in fact, remembered the letters. Perhaps because they did not particularly care to.

It had happened so long ago.

Bayern, the land of their birth, had first claimed the life of their brother, and shortly thereafter it taken that of their father. The night of their father's funeral Kitty had vanished without a word. It was the last the family had ever seen of her, until now. The seven remaining sisters, along with their mother, had soon fled that dark land of sorrowful magic for America, where they tried very hard to be brave. Death comes in threes, they say, and so it must be. Four years after their arrival, Mama was claimed as well. The sisters had found the letters in a drawer in her bedside table. They had been neatly tied together and all of them were unopened.

It had been a bleak and chaotic period of their lives. Thekla had done the right thing in burning the letters, but they all wished she had not opened them before she did so. Kitty had written at length about their brother's death and her great remorse for it. None faulted her for that. But Kitty had sworn to undo it, and that was perilous ground. She seemed obsessed with the past and had penned several long and confusing polemics about space and physics and time. Kitty would somehow restore Louis to them, she had written, and the sisters could not help but be afraid. No one had argued when Thekla declared Kitty insane. They, too, wished Louis had lived, but this was madness. Several of them now glanced at the portrait. Their brother, caught in time, did not say a word.

"Do you think," Elfrieda said at last, "she's found a way?"

"She does possess the gift," Zilli said.

"I will not hear it." Thekla spoke with a conviction she was certain her sisters shared. "The past cannot be changed. It is her Sight that concerns us. The gift you speak of does not make any sense."

Ingeburg sighed. "And what about this family does?"

Thekla snorted her derision. There was nothing wrong with *her* family—it was Kitty who caused all the fuss. She uncrossed her legs and flinched with the pain. Damned arthritis. If anything made no sense, it was that she was finally feeling her years. Blast the drunken ancestor who had given the family the gift of longevity! It was a curse, Thekla thought to herself. She was ninety-four years old and might live another fifty at the rate she was going. *This* was why they gave their gifts so carefully these days. There could not be a repeat of things so thoughtlessly given. Age without health should not be wished on anyone.

Thekla smoothed her skirt over her knees and cleared her throat loudly.

"We can chatter here all night and never find an answer. The gift has been given. There is nothing we can do about that now. My sisters, what we must be considering is how we can stop Kitty's gift from ever manifesting."

Helga and Hilda nodded. They sat next to each other on a brightly colored settee, thighs touching, identical hands resting in identical laps. "She said something about windows breaking," said Helga.

"And fingers pricking," said Hilda.

The twins then spoke thoughtfully in unison, "So we suppose she believes Helena will be killed by something sharp."

"A knife," said Helga.

"Or a sliver of glass," said Hilda.

Thekla almost rolled her eyes at the suggestion. "How have you figured that?"

"How do we figure anything Kitty does?"

"We don't. And we'll never do so from here."

Thekla had an idea, but it would take some doing to bring her sisters into agreement.

Kitty spoiled everything, time after time, Thekla thought. All these years without a word, only the silent terror of knowing she was out there. And then, without warning, she casts her wicked eye our way, as though destroying us once wasn't enough. Thekla remembered the letters, for she had kept the very last one. Addressed solely to her, it was Kitty's attempt to make up for the wrongs of the past, as if a few words could erase all she'd done. Thekla clenched her fists. What right did she think she had?

"Imagine the twins are correct," said Elfrieda. "What then shall we do? Hide every ornament? Keep Helena from the kitchens? Cover all the windows? There is no way to protect her from such a fate, if that is what Kitty has Seen." She crossed and uncrossed her legs, unable to ease the discomfort that was spreading through her knees.

A shadow crossed Thekla's face. "There is a way. We are going to find it."

CHAPTER 3

EVA WOKE WITH A START, HER BODY AWARE THAT MORNING had passed, her mind remaining in that state where all is muted and pale. She sat up and let the sheets wrinkle at her hips, rubbed her blood-shot eyes and fussed with her silver locks before sliding her feet into brocade slippers and heading for the stairs.

She wondered if her sisters had managed to get any rest. Her dreams had been of things rising from the old lake and her sleep had been fitful and uneasy.

It was a foolish—yet daring—plan that Thekla demanded. A return to their ancestral home was begging for another clash with Kitty, and Eva had voiced the loudest arguments against the idea. It was too big. Bayern was too far away. They were too old for the journey. But no, Thekla had insisted. It was the only way.

There was so much to consider, not least that Kitty lived there. Thekla's logic was sound enough. Kitty had the Sight; compared to her, the rest of them were blind. They had to get close to Kitty, or they would never know what she was plotting.

No one denied that Kitty would plot, but Eva hardly thought

they needed to live next door to her as she did it. Thekla had closed her argument nicely: *It is, after all, our home, too.* None of them wanted to admit that those few words moved them as nothing else Thekla said did. They loved their home in America, but Bayern was in their blood.

Eva conceded, but not because she longed for a place she did not remember. The trouble with some gifts is that you cannot tell when or how they will be opened. With a gift such as beauty, all anyone has to do is grow into it, but some gifts linger for years before revealing themselves. They had no way to know when Kitty's gift to Helena would manifest. In Bayern, close to Kitty, they could at least make a more educated guess.

When Eva reached the kitchen she found Elfrieda and Zilli staring into their tea as Ingeburg diced the vine-ripened tomatoes that spilled from a basket nearby. The kitchen was a comfortable place of copper and dark wood, of warmth and quiet contentment. The sisters would be sorry to leave it.

"She gives us a month!" Elfrieda moaned as soon as Eva sat down.

"Hush now," said Zilli kindly, "you've been crying all morning. You'd be better off packing than pining for time you don't have."

Eva poured herself a cup of tea and kept her silence for a moment. Her sisters knew her mind. "Maybe it is for the best," she finally said, but without conviction.

"No one has been there in years! It will be filthy. Not even Thekla can muster the power to have it ready by the time we arrive." More birdlike in her distress than usual, Elfrieda's fingers flitted from teacup to spoon to tomato as she spoke. She would not be calmed.

Eva could only shake her head at her sister; the state of the house was the last thing on Thekla's mind. *All beauty and no brains*, she thought, though not unkindly.

Ingeburg turned and waved her knife in the air. "A change of scenery will do us all good, and don't you forget," here she aimed at Elfrieda, "our priority is the child." She returned to the board and diced an onion with a flash of her hand.

Helga and Hilda walked into the room, fresh from a stroll through the garden where they'd plucked a fragrant array of roses. Helga reached for a vase while Hilda spoke softly to Hope, requesting a loaf of bread and a hunk of cheese and a bowl of soup for Helga. Each made herself a place at the table and immediately began to voice their opinions about the month ahead.

"It is not enough time," Helga said.

"What will we do with this house?" Hilda asked anyone who might know the answer.

"Sell it, I imagine." Ingeburg said. None of them would ever return to America once they'd left it. The upheaval was too much for them. At their ages, they should be settled down. Ingeburg laughed loudly, much to Elfrieda's dismay.

"What do you find so amusing?"

Ingeburg couldn't hold in a final chuckle. "Imagine us, world travelers. They won't know what to think when we board the plane. We shall look, dare I say it, most surreal."

"Plane?" Elfrieda had visions of an ocean liner, steaming over the sea.

It was Zilli's turn to laugh. "A new age has dawned out there. Of course we are going to fly."

"With the baby?" All eyes turned to Hope, who shrugged and said nothing.

Eva listened as her sisters continued to bicker about their impending journey. None of them mentioned why they were going, as though that part of it could be overlooked.

She hated to bring up the matter of their sister, but felt it had to be done.

"I still believe it to be a bad idea. We could at least take up residence in the city. We have no real need to be that close to Kitty." Eva knew, even as she spoke, that she was wrong.

The sisters fell silent. Even Hope momentarily stopped what she was doing and waited to see who would answer.

"But we do," said Zilli sadly. "She has the advantage."

"Still, she won't trouble us again, will she?" Elfrieda tucked one of her curls behind her ear. As the youngest, she was used to being treated somewhat differently than the others—more gently, as though she were still a child. She was shocked by their honesty.

"Yes." All of the others drew out the word, as though they each had the same thought at the same time, but only grudgingly voiced it.

"You can be sure of it," Eva added.

Ingeburg stabbed the cutting board with the knife, embedding it into the wood upright like a soldier standing at attention. The women jumped and put hands to hearts or mouths as their eyes snapped to the blade. The roses the twins had gathered shook briefly. A moment of quiet descended as one crimson petal fell, through sun and through shadow, gracefully onto the table.

"We will just have to do our best to protect our own," Ingeburg said. "Like it or not, we are going."

Eva frowned at the flowers. She might not remember much about their old home, but one thing could not be forgotten. A fearsome thicket of roses, black and bare, wrapped the house in a net of decay. The family had tried to cut them out and destroy them, but the land would not let them die. They grew back—blackened and grasping, but never blooming— every time. Eva shuddered and pulled her robe tightly around her.

"Hope, what do you know of roses?" Eva wondered how Hope would react when she saw them.

Hope believed Eva's question to be rhetorical, but she answered her anyway. "I know how to grow them and I know how to cut them back."

"We may have use for that knowledge, I'm afraid. Especially when it comes to the cutting." Eva tapped her fingers on the table. "May I ask you something, Ingeburg?"

"Of course you may."

"Is it possible?"

Ingeburg sighed. "Anything is possible, Eva. If you are asking me if it is probable, I have to say no, it is not. You know how these things operate. No future is fixed as the present unfolds, but the past has been fossilized."

Yes, Eva thought, *but Kitty's gift was* time.

CHAPTER 4

KITTY WAS NOT FOND OF FLYING. SHE PREFERRED TO WALK when she had to travel, though for Kitty *travel* more often meant moving from her bed to a comfortable seat. She swore never to board an aircraft again, and was very glad when her feet had touched the solid ground of home. She gratefully settled her aching bones into her favorite plush chair as Karl, her friend and attendant, carried her bag upstairs. She took a moment and stretched it out until it met forever, then turned her mind toward the preparations. When Karl returned, she explained what was happening. He shook his head.

"You've invited your family here?" He could not believe it. Fifteen years he'd worked for Katza, and not once had a single soul come to call.

"I didn't invite them, young man. I simply know they are coming." She winked as he took a notepad and pen from his pocket and began to commit her instructions to paper.

The family's ancestral home had remained mostly untended after Mama had sailed off with Kitty's sisters. When Kitty, alone, had returned to the house, she found she could not live in it. She instead had the old coach house refurbished and transformed into a home. It lay on the far side of the courtyard and was now neatly hidden behind saplings, brush, and old trees whose branches should have been pruned years ago. The stable nearby had fallen into ruin.

Gone were the days when the whole family had gathered, and parties and balls had been held almost weekly in summer months. The courtyard, once full of coaches and horses and grooms running to contain them, was a lonely and silent place where weeds grew in the cracks between flagstones. Birds nested where tack had once hung in the stable, and the main kitchen garden was fully overgrown.

Karl kept the lawns trimmed and the flowers watered, but there was no reason to maintain a large garden with no one there to use it. That would soon change.

The interior of the great house had faded over time and its muslin-draped furniture was layered with decades of dust. Kitty could not bear to enter the house; it held too many reminders of Louis, her long-dead brother. The house had been asleep these many years. It would be good to have life restored to it.

"We have a great deal of work ahead of us," Kitty said as Karl held his pen at the ready. "And not much time to do it in. You'll have to call the agency, have them send you some help. Have the cellar swept and one wine-rack filled. The first and second floors must be dusted and swept and the furniture uncovered. All of the silver must be polished—I won't have them thinking I've not taken care of Mother's things. And that kitchen is a disgrace. They'll want one of those American refrigerators, I'm sure. And don't forget to weed and turn the soil in the kitchen garden, and cut back the hedge. That should do it. If they want to plant there, they can do it themselves."

There was nothing they could do about the roses. Her sisters would just have to live with them, as she did.

Kitty, finished with this bit of business, tiredly climbed the narrow stair and passed through a dim hall until she reached the large bedroom at its end. There she pushed the switch and sighed as the familiar sight of her linens, pulled smartly around the edge of the mattress, appeared in the light. The worst thing about traveling was sleeping in an unfamiliar bed.

The long hours of the flight, spent cramped amidst plastic and impatient strangers, had taken their toll. Kitty pulled back the sheets with a whoosh and inhaled the pinching scent of starch like a breath of clean air.

Beyond the window, the stars shone down upon the main house. They illuminated, just barely, the briars wrapped around its foundation, where for almost one hundred years not a single rose had bloomed.

ℴℴ

The following weeks were pleasantly warm and the breeze carried daily the scent of the lake that bordered the grounds to the west. Kitty reclined in a wicker chair, her thick braids wrapped around the top of her head and her hands folded in her lap, waiting. Her eyes were closed, but in the deep dark behind her lids she saw the lake as it had been in her youth, before the cross was placed in the water, as if a reminder of suffering could somehow give them all ease.

A memory surfaced; she was kneeling in the grass, spreading

a quilt below the limbs of a tree. It was her birthday. Standing beside her, a young man with an Alpine face and tight, black curls held a basket of wine and bread. It was Louis.

She felt a spider of fear cross the nape of her neck, as though it were happening again. She reached up and repositioned her braids, touched the pins to establish their whereabouts and then dropped her hands back into her lap.

She had loved him so much. Quiet, self-assured, polite: he was everything a girl could want in a brother and she never dreamed she would live her life without him. Kitty could relive the day of his death at any time. She choked, gasped quietly for air and clung to the wicker arms of the chair to steady herself. Her Sight had failed her—*she* had failed to See it coming. The blame for his death lay on her shoulders like a lead shawl that could not be shrugged off. Kitty exhaled and forced herself to relax. She would not need her Sight now. Now she had hindsight, the clearest vision of all.

ജ

Louis had been born to Magdalena and Louis the elder in the year 1868, the first of nine children and their only boy. Two years later, on a fine day in June, blind Katza had been born and the pair became instantly inseparable. When Katza began to crawl on her knees, Louis had stayed by her side, guiding her away from furniture and stairs. When she began to walk, it had been Louis who held her hand and led her through the gardens, plucked flowers from their stems and held them to her nose. It was Louis who had first sat her on the back of a horse and climbed up behind to hold her in place. He had been a gentle boy who seemed to know that his small sister could not see the world as he did.

When Katza fell from the horse on that dreadful day, he had been the one to carry her into the house. As she had slept in her weeklong coma, Louis had remained by her bed. When she opened her eyes, his face had been the first thing she saw. By the time Magdalena bore Thekla, one year later, Katza and Louis had been tangled together like vines.

Their childhood had been framed by the seasons. When winter swarmed over the forest the two had stayed inside the great house. There they had explored each hallway and closet they could find. It was an old house; the wood was dark and thick and mysterious swirls rippled up the paneling like waves. The floors were of marble or stone or covered in carpets from the east. They had hidden from each other in the tall curtains and were delighted to find behind one a secret stair. It led to a small room with a thin, boarded-up window, and a single mirror hanging on the wall. They had spent hours guessing at its purpose, or peering into the mist of its silver surface to see what might come out of its tarnished depths.

In summer they had stolen away from lessons and wandered the forest, run through the fields, and laid in the shade by the lake, beneath the old oak that stretched lopsided over the water. It seemed even then he'd been drawn to the water, as though he somehow understood that his destiny lay beneath the waves. Papa had built a swing on the tree's thickest limb and Louis had spent hours sending Katza into the sky.

Louis would bring Katza roses plucked from the bushes

surrounding the house, great falling armloads of them, red and lush, and string the petals in her hair. She would wrinkle her nose to pretend annoyance, but he'd been her sun and moon.

Things had changed as they grew. Louis had begun to hide from Katza; he turned his face from her and spent all of his time alone. Sometimes, as she had walked the garden paths, she would see him in the distance, a cold and solitary figure stalking the hills or riding hard down the lane. It had cut her deeply; for two long years Katza ate the pain of abandonment. Her special Sight had offered no clues to his behavior, only visions of her brother riding through the woods and away. She had waited for him to return to her, until at last she could stand no more.

"Where have you gone?" she had asked him, trapping him neatly by the door to the stable where the scent of fresh hay filled the air. The horses had shuffled and blew hot breath out of black nostrils, disturbing the mounds of dirt in the corners of their stalls. "I won't leave until I get an answer."

At the look on his face, she had flung herself into his arms.

"Katza," he'd said as he stroked her hair, and she had known all would be well again. Two years of silence interrupted by the sound of her name.

"Louis," she wept, "why do you hide from me?"

"Oh Katza," he'd whispered into her hair, "I am in love."

She had tensed in his arms as something folded up inside of her.

"But surely this is a good thing," she had said, once the shock subsided.

"It is no thing," he'd replied. "It is not a love that can ever be fulfilled."

"Why not?" Katza, then and now, believed that anything should be possible. "Don't worry, Mama will arrange matters."

Louis had almost laughed at the innocent comment. "No, in this matter I'm afraid even Mama's connections won't help."

"Who is it?" she had asked, drawing away from him, glancing at him from the corner of her eye, looking for subtle changes she may have missed. May have seen and misunderstood.

He shrugged and let his arms fall to his sides. "It doesn't matter. My love cannot be returned."

She had taken a step toward him and tried to put her hand on his lapel.

Louis had backed away from her. "Let us not speak of it. It is a fancy of mine, nothing more." He crossed his arms over his chest.

Katza had bit her tongue (she recalled the pain well) and laid a hand on his elbow. "Do not keep yourself away from me," she had said.

He'd taken her hand in his. "I am right here."

She had nodded. She had believed she understood. Her brother would soon come to his senses.

All she had to do was wait.

∞ ∞

Kitty shifted in her chair as she remembered that day and the look on her brother's face. It was a natural gift of age, to be better able to recall the far past than what had happened a moment ago. Kitty's memory was sharp as a needle. Every detail was enshrined there and she visited almost daily. She thought she'd grow used to the pain over time, but she hadn't. It remained fresh as ever, a wound she could not let heal. Louis, her brother, had not come to his senses. Instead, he had lost them all.

CHAPTER 5

THE WINTER FOLLOWING THEIR REUNION, LOUIS AND KATZA
had spent many fine hours sharing a seat, talking and reading
and watching the snow fall beyond the wide windows of the
house. Despite his strange mood, she had been overjoyed to
have Louis to herself again.

They were together the night a terrible blizzard had swept in.
Louis had said the wind was the result of a giant roaring on
top of the Alps. Katza had laughed; no fell or fantastic creature
could harm her with Louis at her side. They had watched as
the snow clumped on the branches and filled up the sills, ice
spreading, root-like, on the glass. Louis had tucked a blanket
around Katza's knees before going into the kitchen to fetch
two steaming cups of cocoa. The house had been quiet;
everyone was in bed, where all good people belong at such an
hour. Katza had snuggled into the settee. At that moment, her
life was painfully perfect.

When Louis did not return as soon as she thought he
should, Katza had unwillingly pulled herself up and gone in
search of him. The house had groaned around her. The night
lamps made small crescents of light in the hall, but did nothing
to dispel the ghosts lurking in dark corners and doorways. A

heavy feeling had grown in her stomach. Though it teased and tugged at her, she could not discern its source.

She had reached the entrance to the kitchens and stopped. From beyond the door she'd heard the sound of men talking quietly among themselves. Their voices were deep and calm, but she could not make out the words. As she pushed open the door, shock had rippled through her body and caught her there on the threshold. Three faces had turned toward her. Louis' features fell readily into place, but she could not believe in the man who had been in the room with him. Even had she *Seen* this, she would not have believed.

There, at the great table where Cook prepared the food, stood their mercurial monarch, King Ludwig II. Behind him an attendant cast his eyes around the room, but Katza saw only the king. Snow had melted from their cloaks and slid down their boots, creating little lakes of fresh water on the stone floor at their feet. Katza had stuttered and coughed and then fled, running as though a monster was chasing behind her. She knew who her brother loved and it was impossible.

Katza had flailed through the corridors, her white dressing gown billowing about her legs, turning her into one of the fleeting ghosts she had so recently imagined. She had run blindly until she came to a stop, trembling, before the curtains concealing the hidden stair. Her hands had run down the edges of the fabric as she parted them. She turned the cold, brass doorknob. Each action had brought another shock to bear on her shaking frame. The years with Louis, the years without him, and the short time she'd had him again all jerked like badly made marionettes in front of her eyes.

She could not recall her feet landing on any step, but Katza would never forget what she had Seen in the mirror that hung in the secret room. A face, old and lined, with great waves of silver hair falling down around it, had peered out from the spotted glass. The eyes had stared into Katza's own, as though the old woman had known she was there. *It must be one of my spells*, Katza had thought, *the Sight upon me again.* She had been caught in time, frozen in place by the sound of the woman's voice.

Break the spell, the woman in the mirror had said.

The small room had spun. Strips of faded and peeling wallpaper seemed to wave about as though a wind gusted through the walls. Katza lost her balance, felt her feet turn in and a sharp pain as her hip hit the floor. As she slipped into unconsciousness, the last thing she'd seen had been the old woman's weary face. She was smiling.

☙ ❧

When Katza woke the next day, she might have thought she had dreamt the scene except she was prone on a cold floor with that voice still in her ears. *What spell?* It was easier to think about that than the other thing she had seen. Louis could not love another and he certainly could not love Ludwig. He was supposed to love her, his devoted sister, not their lunatic king.

She had eased herself upright and shook out her gown, run a hand over the remains of her braid and taken a painful step toward the door. She did not know how to face that new day, but it could not be ignored.

She had reached her room, where the bed's four posters seemed to mock her: they stood at attention, perfectly vertical, while she slouched past, bent with shame. She had felt heavy and hollow—both at the same time—as though she might faint again at any moment and crash through the floor to land on some poor soul below.

Katza had refused to give in to it. She'd found her robe and thrown it over her shoulders, ripped out her braid in a fury of combing and drawn a very deep breath.

Louis had caught her just as she was leaving her room.

"Katza," he said.

"Louis." What else could she have said? Her eyes had narrowed as she noted the changes the night had wrought in her brother. Her name on his lips meant nothing. He had reached out a hand, cold as bone, for one of hers.

"Please don't tell anyone who you saw here last night. He has requested our silence."

Katza had looked away from her brother as she let his hand go. "I'll say nothing, but not for his sake. For yours."

Damn Ludwig's midnight rides anyway. They were not peasants! Why had he chosen to darken their door that night? Katza had closed the door to her bedroom and left Louis alone in the hall.

₭ℂ

I was a fool, Kitty thought, returning her mind to the present. There was still much to be done and while the renovations of the main house were well underway, Kitty had one final thing to attend to. She roused herself and waved at Karl who stood nearby.

"Have you hung it?"

Karl's face was like stone. "Yes, I have."

The task had not been easy to complete, for he was no longer so young himself, but she'd insisted he handle it alone. A spare lantern had gone first and then his tools, and then finally he'd hefted the mirror up the hidden, narrow stairwell. Karl, ever a practical man, had begun to think the stairway might be haunted. Each time he'd traveled the passage it appeared to end in a different place. The door was the same, but when he opened it he swore he saw mountains, or a lake, or even fields of golden wheat spread out beyond the walls. It had unnerved him. Though not prone to hysteria, Karl had done the unthinkable and broken one of Kitty's laws.

Disturb nothing in that room, she had said. *Not one speck of dust should be moved.* He dared not tell her, but he'd opened a small window set high in the wall. It had been sealed and boarded over long before for reasons forgotten by now.

It had been the most difficult thing he'd ever done.

As he'd begun to pry at the piece of wood covering the single-paned window, he'd been overcome by an intense feeling of déjà vu, as though everything he was about to do, he'd already done. Karl had *known* that within moments, he would find himself unable to go against Kitty's wishes. He had known the argument he would have with himself. He had known how the fears raised by that strange, little room would war with his loyalty toward his employer and that he would step away from the window, leaving it sealed.

Karl had found himself shaking as the moment passed. He had taken a deep breath to steady himself when, with a horrible abruptness, a large and oddly marked spider appeared on the windowsill in front of him. His heart, he later claimed, had nearly stopped.

That's it, Karl thought. *Kitty will never know.*

He simply had to let in some light to dispel the ghosts in that room and yet, the more he thought of removing the wooden barrier, the more his sense of déjà vu had worked against him.

Finally, in a moment of mental anguish, he'd ripped the old wood away from the glass with a grunt and a twist of his arms. As light found its way through the old, dirty window, Karl had sighed with relief. He'd hung the mirror and fled the room and he never wanted to go there ever again.

℅℞

"Well?"

Karl blinked. "Excuse me, did you say something?"

Kitty glared. "Have you locked the door?"

"Oh, yes." He fumbled in his jacket pocket and pulled out a small, silver key. "Here you are."

Kitty took the key, held it in her hand, turned it over and smiled.

Clenching the key in her fist, reassured by its hard metal, she dismissed Karl with another wave and then stomped off to her room. The brass lamp on her vanity table gave off a wan light as she dumped a box of jewelry out onto its hardwood surface. Her fingers sifted through pearls and garnets until she found the thin chain she sought. She threaded the key onto it and clasped it around her neck, and then sat. The dim light revealed stacks of books piled randomly about the legs of her dressing table. She pulled a blue-bound volume from the heap beside her chair. She knew its contents well, for she'd read it far into many nights, until her eyes ached, memorizing the passages contained in its brittle pages.

A portion of the family's genealogy was recorded in the book, along with a description of the gifts each person had received and in some cases, how those gifts had manifested. This volume covered her generation and those younger. She frowned to see her own name there, faded with age, her gift of *time* beside it with a question mark, as though whoever recorded her gift had not quite understood what it was. Kitty penned in Helena's date of birth—13 June 1970. She cackled to herself as she listed Helena's gifts beside her name, and then she shut the book and put it aside.

All she could do now was wait, but Kitty did not mind. Life was full of waiting. She was good at it by now.

CHAPTER 6

THE PUNGENT SCENT OF DAMP SPRUCE WAFTED THROUGH the open window of Thekla's bedroom. She stretched her arms as best as she could and opened her eyes, overcome for a moment with a feeling of disorientation. She rose from her bed and went to the window. Thekla's belly pressed into the sill as she craned her neck, trying to fit the whole sweep of the countryside into her vision, inhaling deeply of its aroma. Bayern, dark and magical land—she was home.

Her sisters had been delighted at their first sight of the house, more impressive than they'd imagined, more familiar than they'd hoped. Even Thekla had crowded in with a secret relief. The house was a jettied, four-story manor, traditionally half-timbered with crossing dark beams that drew the eye toward the steep, slated roof. It was solid and stout and surrounded on three sides by the imposing forest. The courtyard was behind the house, while the grounds spread out in front, a calm sea of lawn dotted with a sparse scattering of trees, as though they had staggered out of the forest one-by-one and taken root. The lawn bordered the lake in which Louis had drowned. One of several drawbacks, Thekla thought callously, that could not be avoided.

There were eight separate bedrooms on the second floor, with doorways of dark wood interrupting the pattern on the papered walls. Kitty's old bedroom was at the front of the house, tucked into the far corner of the north wing. Helena now slept there. Thekla's bedroom was at the back of the house. The lake could not be seen from the windows, but the hedge of black thorns was visible below the sills. In Thekla's youth the scent of roses had filled the air from early spring until the end of autumn, when the first frost covered the ground. The day Louis died, every last bloom had withered on its stem, as though they couldn't live without him either—like Papa, who perished shortly after. All that was left was the memory of scent, etched onto the naked limbs of the briars that clung stubbornly to the house. Thekla, old now and as barren as the roses, wondered how long it would be before she, too, was no more than memory, a phrase carved into stone.

The roses had caused quite a stir when the sisters arrived. Thekla had to explain, over and over, that there was nothing they could do. The blackened stems were embedded in the landscape, a part of the house itself, and nothing they did would make them bloom or force them to disappear. They had to live with them, she had told her sisters, and then refused to speak again for the rest of the day.

Thekla had been more horrified when, upon entering the house for the first time in years, they found everything in order for their arrival. The curtains were fresh and the woodwork glowed from a polishing. Paintings had been carefully un-covered and dusted, carpets had been swept and upon every bed the sheets were tucked in tightly. Thekla had fumed and stormed for several days, muttering to any who would listen about how it was all Kitty's evil doing. She'd even scowled at the new light switches. They couldn't have been installed in a month. Thekla was furious.

One week later, there was still evidence of the confusion they'd brought with them scattered throughout the house. In the hallway Thekla bumped her knee against a box of trinkets Zilli would not leave behind. She muttered at her sister's carelessness as she made her way into the kitchen, where Hope was preparing breakfast for them all.

The kitchen was an immaculate fortress of pots and pans, all hung in a glistening array from stout beams in the ceiling. Thekla had watched Hope peek into the cupboards on the day of their arrival. Hope's pleasure in finding them stocked with clean dishes, cups, foodstuffs and a hodge-podge of sundries had been obvious. When she'd checked the pantry, it seemed Hope would faint at the wealth it contained. Thekla's eyes had narrowed in anger, but even she had to agree that the new freezer was impressive.

Thekla kissed Helena, who was propped up in her high chair with a pillow, before pouring a cup of steaming black coffee into a sturdy clay mug. Hope dusted her floury hands on her apron and began to set out bowls full of applesauce, eggs, melon, and toast. Thekla smiled her thanks as Helena conversed in burps and squeals with Hope or the tableware or with anything she thought would listen. Breakfast was consumed to the sounds of Hope's rolling pin thumping on the dough, Helena's angry chirping, and the clink of Thekla's fork against a china plate. The others would come in, singly or in pairs, as the morning passed. Thekla was glad for a moment of peace before they did so.

She had, at last, allowed herself to appreciate the simple joy of being home. She had admired the delicate Persian rugs and the velvet curtains and pushed aside the thought that Kitty herself might have chosen the fabrics. Thekla, with no way to know that Karl had chosen new furnishings and restored the old, had drifted between outrage and enjoyment as she wended through the rooms, down the hallways and up the stairs, returning the home to memory. In the music room, she had shut the door to make sure no one could see her and then sat down, eyes hot with tears. Though it was no longer there, she could still see the old piano in the corner.

Thekla dabbed at her eyes with a napkin as those same tears threatened again. She glanced at Hope, and was relieved to find her turned away. She would not like to be caught in a moment of raw emotion.

The piano had been a baby grand. Its ivory keys had called to Thekla from the moment she could reach them. She had been taught to read music, but she'd never needed those straight lines and harsh notations in order to play. As soon as her father had sat her on the bench, her fingers had picked out a tune. Her lessons had started in earnest and continued even during the awful period after Louis died. She'd been a wonder to hear; no human hands should be able to draw such sounds from an instrument.

When they'd moved to America, the piano had been left behind, put in storage. It would be out of tune by now, she thought, dulled by the passage of time and grown small with age like the rest of them. It had been replaced by a grand piano in the family's new home, where Thekla had continued her lessons with a different instructor. Playing had been her passion, her healing, and her escape. Her first great performance had been scheduled; she had been billed as a prodigy and assured of a wonderful future. But it was that evening, shortly before the concert was to begin, that their mother had been found dead.

Kitty should have been there for them, Thekla had thought for the thousandth time, but Kitty had been here, in that filthy coach house, making impossible plans to change the past while avoiding the present entirely.

Thekla, bound by obligation, had taken over the care of her sisters and never touched a piano again. She had pushed all of her sorrow down into those places it is best kept, in the dark and secret corners of the heart where it troubles no one but itself. Giving Helena her own gift of music had woken it up again.

Thekla's thoughts turned again to Kitty, who had thrown obligation to the wind on more than this one occasion. No, there were even older bones to pick with Kitty. She interfered when she was not wanted and vanished when she was needed, every single time.

Helena threw her spoon across the table, startling Hope and forcing Thekla back to the here and now. Thekla rose, a decision abruptly made. She was going to pay her elder sister a visit. She did not mean to offer a truce, for there could be none between them. Thekla went only to demand that Kitty stay out of their lives.

ॐ◯ও

"I know you planned for this," Thekla said at Kitty's doorway, refusing to cross the threshold. "We are here. You may leave us alone now."

Kitty coughed. "I have no intention of disturbing you or our sisters. They know where to find me if they have a need."

Thekla shook her head. "We did not come here for you, but in the hopes of undoing what you have done."

"I know."

Thekla refused to react, though she could feel the familiar anger bubbling in her gut. "You are to leave the child alone."

"Do you think to order me about as you do the rest of our sisters?" Kitty chuckled. "I will do as I please."

"You always have." Thekla spat before walking away.

Thekla crossed the courtyard and left Kitty's house behind her. She hoped never to have to return.

The forest was close all around, not the straggling trees that adorned the grounds but the thick, wild wood where Louis had once hunted. At the edge of the flagstones she walked under the pergola that bordered the garden wall. It dripped with a froth of clematis and dark ivy that had wound its way up the stones. The tunnel ended at a small wooden door in a frame of crumbling stones.

"I'll have to put a lock on this door," Thekla muttered as she pulled it open. "I won't have that woman thinking she can stroll over here whenever she likes."

Beyond lay the kitchen gardens, where a bench invited her to rest. Thekla felt needles of pain shoot through her knees. A moment will not hurt, she thought as she lowered herself onto the hard seat with a sigh. She was too old for this nonsense. Perhaps they should face Kitty's gift and maybe, if they were lucky, that would be an end to it. But how to face something you don't fully understand?

"I must be mad, to think such a thing," Thekla said out loud. She blamed Kitty; the sight of her had caused Thekla to lose all reason. Family drew family in these dark woods, but until the christening, it had been years since she'd seen Kitty's face. There in that room recognition had been instinctive and at Kitty's door, it had happened just so, again. Thekla's body had tensed and her breath had come in short bursts from her lungs. Kitty was a ghost come to life and Thekla was done with being haunted.

The past began to circle Thekla as she sat in the quiet garden. Unlike Katza, she didn't like to look too closely at it. She usually summed up history concisely: Louis died and Katza left. She did not dwell on the myriad of emotions that lurked just to the side of those words. She was afraid of those emotions and afraid of what she'd become if she acknowledged them. Thekla had to be strong for her sisters; she had to hold what was left of the family together. Though she felt old and tired, she knew now was no time to weaken.

CHAPTER 7

KITTY SULKED AFTER THEKLA LEFT. SHE FELT NO REMORSE for anything she'd done after her brother's death. It was what she hadn't done to prevent it that plagued her. Thekla judged her and found her lacking, but her sisters would never know the truth about Louis, gods willing, nor should they. They all believed his death was accidental—he drowned, no more than that. Their mother, Magdalena, had made it clear. Kitty's younger sisters were never to know how or why it had happened. Kitty sighed. Even Mama had not known all of the ugly truth.

The deaths had occurred so quickly. First the king murdered, then Louis drowned, and before Kitty could come to terms with either, her father had died of sorrow for both. Her Sight was useless, she had thought at the time, but her other gift was suddenly not—if only she knew how to use it. She had left home, determined to find a way.

Kitty recalled those days with displeasure. She had done nothing but waste precious time in the end and she, of all people, should have known better. Youth, it is true, is wasted on the young.

When the rest of the family moved to America without

her, Kitty had returned to their home. The answers she had been seeking had been there all along.

At first she had wandered aimlessly through the rooms and hallways as her feet traced the pattern in the carpets, recalling the route they'd once followed beside another pair of larger, surer feet. Louis' feet. When she could no longer bear the reminders of her brother in every dusty corner, she had turned the coach house into a place where memory would be close, but not so stifling.

It was during the process of closing down the great house that she had found again the hidden stair and recalled the words the hag had spoken on the night of the king's visit.

Break the spell—Kitty had known then with a sudden, piercing pain, what the old woman had meant.

Once realized, it seemed so obvious that Kitty had raged for days at her own stupidity. Her brother would never have loved the king of his own accord; Ludwig must have enchanted him. The hag had been telling *her* to break his spell. It had been another shock to imagine the hag was herself, in the distant future, warning herself about Ludwig. Was it a future in which Louis lived or died? She could not know for certain, but there was one thing of which she'd been sure.

An enchantment was the answer. In Bayern the land itself is magic, and no king ever loved his land as much as Ludwig II. He was a dreamer and in dreams magic is made. Her family had been loyal and all loved their monarch deeply, in the way that subjects will. But Louis' love—she was certain—had been born of magic. It was unnatural, and it had caused him to do unnatural things.

Yes, Thekla and the others could hate her all they liked. It hardly mattered now. Only she knew Ludwig's secret and saw how it fit into the rest of her brother's tale. There was no need for her sisters to learn the truth. Kitty smiled, her foul mood passed.

All Kitty needed was time, and she had plenty of it.

CHAPTER 8

TIME HAS A STRANGE WAY OF PASSING—BLINK AND A DAY becomes years. Before the sisters knew it, Helena was walking and talking and had grown taller than their knees. Ink marked the moments to be recalled and diaries were filled with elaborate descriptions of Helena's many achievements. The aunts adored her, for in her they saw all that was good in themselves and if they spoiled her just a little, it was only done out of love.

Helena's gifts quickly revealed themselves. She was a supple girl, sleek of skin and hair, whose eyelids hung low and dark lashes turned up and when she smiled a dimple appeared in the corner of her cheek. Intelligent and charming, it was difficult for her aunts to resist the gifts they themselves had given her. Her doctor, who called monthly, gave up on his charts as Helena surpassed all the statistics he knew. Her tutors, some of the best the continent could offer, were astonished to find she could often outsmart them. The aunts shared triumphant smiles, knowing themselves entirely responsible for Helena's apparent perfection.

She grew like an impossible, beautiful weed. Yet as her aunts' generous gifts flourished, they seemed to drain Helena of other, perhaps more necessary, nutrients—essential elements such as empathy or concern. Helena was a product of her gifts; as much a homunculus as any lump of animated dirt and like such, she seemed to lack a soul or any part that could be considered of it.

Her aunts would see no wrong in her. If she shouted or threw the butter-knife, why, that was just a tantrum or a mood. The doctor called them growing pains. He knew better than to argue and since the child's physical health was excellent, he kept his concerns for those late nights when only the stars heard him utter complaints.

Tutors fled from bites to the hand or kicks to the shin; one had a book flung at his head because he wouldn't read a story quickly enough for her. Helena wooed them all with her grace and charm, but there was only so much they could take. The sisters simply shook their heads and increased their pay, or sent them out with an extra bribe in exchange for their silence. Helena sat in the center as always, while around her the household slowly fell into disarray.

Her episodes were not the result of moods or growing pains, nor were they simple tantrums. As a result of her gifts, Helena was aware of herself. This little girl knew precisely what she was made of—eight parts in equal measure and not one thing more.

All eight were painful masters, for all had a ravenous need. Music demanded music; she would play until her fingers bled if the other parts would let her, but song demanded song. By the end of each day her voice was hoarse, yet dance demanded dance and so it went. At least Helena could feed these, for she knew what they required. Not so her eighth part. That she could not name. She knew she was made of song and dance, of beauty and wit, of grace and finally, of death. *How* she'd been made she did not understand, but that did not concern her. The need to know and sate her eighth part ruled Helena's world.

℘℆

It was a day like any other in late summer. The air was crisp, the birds were singing and the flowers were in bloom, but for the roses. Helena was in the kitchen garden under the watchful eyes of Hope, who was never to let the child out of her sight when they were outdoors. Hope's apron waved in a breeze as she bent over a bed of mint while Helena, left to her own devices, skipped down a path and stopped at the hedge at its end. Once, she imagined, the path went on to wind through the roses. Now the hedge blocked the way. She parted its branches and ducked underneath where the bloomless roses grew in a dank mass of blackened stems.

The briars held a secret tight by their thorns and Helena wanted to know it. She closed her hand upon a stem, opened it and gazed at the blood on her palm where one of the thorns had pricked her. She was studying the smear when she heard something fall onto the path behind her. She crawled back below the hedge and saw, amidst the leaves and twigs on the stone, the body of a tiny bird. It fluttered a wing and opened its beak; it was still alive.

"Hope! Come look!" she shouted.

"What's this? Where have you been?" Hope reached Helena's

side, saw the bird and frowned. "The poor thing. I'm sorry, Helena, but there is nothing we can do."

Helena looked up at Hope, who shuddered at what she saw in the child's eyes.

A gift roared. Helena stood and before Hope could stop her, she brought her foot down on the little bird.

"It's dead," Helena sang in her childish voice. "I did it."

Hope stood as still as stone until Helena touched her, and then she shuddered again. "Come, Helena," she said, as if to a wild beast. "We must go in now."

Helena shrugged. She did not expect Hope to understand.

She allowed Hope to wash her hands in the sink and then went in search of Thekla, who was found napping beside a small, bright fire in the library. Even in the heat of summer, Thekla's legs were always cold. Her feet were shod in thick, black shoes and crossed each other neatly, but the stockings gathered around her ankles dispersed the illusion of dignity she tried to maintain. Helena's vision was always full of shoes. She knew every pair her grandaunts owned and could count the numbers of eyelets in each by memory.

She put a hand on Thekla's knee. "Aunt," she said, and watched Thekla spring up, grasping for composure.

"You gave me quite a fright, young lady." Thekla leaned forward and brushed a twig from Helena's shoulder. "Have you been outdoors with Hope?"

"How else would there be sticks in my hair?" Helena shook her head. Adults loved to question the obvious. Her question was better than that.

No one liked to talk about death or to be reminded of

its existence. Even the doctor had nothing to say; he knew only how to keep his customers from it. She was hushed and shushed and patted on the head until she felt she would burst with the well-meaning ignorance of everyone around her. They did not understand that death held a clue as to what her eighth part might be.

"I was wondering, Aunt. How do things die?"

Thekla froze. Not this again. The air coalesced around them; neither moved. Thekla thought she saw roses blooming in Helena's eyes.

"It is a natural process, Helena," she finally said. "Everything living must die when its time comes. What's gotten into you? You're too young to ask such questions."

"No. I'm not."

Helena watched Thekla inspect her face. Helena was inscrutable, immovable, and impossible to challenge and she knew it, but she didn't expect Thekla to be taken in by her charm, not this time.

"Yes, you most certainly are."

Helena ignored her aunt's show of defiance. "Who decides when it's time?"

"Time for what?"

Helena rolled her eyes. "Time to die."

Thekla's face hardened into a stern mask. "Only the gods can make that decision, and we do not question them. That is enough now," she said. "Don't trouble yourself with thoughts of death. It will be many years yet before your own time comes, if that's what you're worried about."

"I'm not worried about anything," Helena said, and left.

It was true. Thekla's answer had changed everything.

Helena was made of death and could therefore choose its moment, as she had with the bird when she squashed it. This she already knew. But according to Thekla, this made her a god, and that she had never suspected.

Helena was uncertain about the matter of gods. The sky was allegedly populated with them, so many that she wondered they had any room to themselves. People prayed to them, made offerings to them, and danced for them under the moon. If the gods answered their pleas, she did not know. They did not seem to have much of a purpose, their existence had yet to be proven and she had always thought she would wait and see for herself if they were more than myth. Now Helena suddenly numbered among them and in her aunts had her very own followers.

She might have reveled in this notion, were she a different girl, but to Helena it meant only one thing. She had already noted that life and death are inseparable. She'd watched seeds become food that perished under Hope's quick knife. She had already reasoned that since death was one part of her, then life might just be one, too. Until now, she'd been unable to confirm this. But gods could personify both life and death, and they dealt equally well in both. And since she was a god, she could do the same. Helena clapped her hands together and laughed. She'd been right all along!

Her eighth part *must* be life.

Joy soon succumbed to logic, however. In order to feed life she would have to create life, but Helena was not so omnipotent. Planting seeds, she knew, was not the same as creating the seeds to be planted. Her hands fell to her sides. Despite knowing its name, she still could not feed her eighth part through the use of it. Either something was still missing or she was wrong, and the latter was simply not possible. She held the Grail of her short existence in her hand. It was empty.

As with any god, her followers would eventually enshrine her, cover her with incense and flowers, and ossify her beneath their perfume. Attention would be lavished upon her, she would sing and dance as she pleased, and wear only the finest clothes money could buy. She was a god who knew nothing beyond her own mountain, did not even know of the fire surrounding it. Around her old women plotted and schemed, but gods never notice their followers' troubles when they have their own problems to solve.

So they went, some on the path of devotion and some on the path of fear, guarding Helena who stayed safe in her temple, trying to feed a hunger that grew larger by the day.

CHAPTER 9

THE COLD FINGER OF SUSPICION DREW ITS BONY TIP ACROSS Thekla's brow, spelled out a name in the wrinkles of her skin. *Kitty.* It had to be some working of her gift. Why else would Helena be having such morbid thoughts? Thekla prayed they were not too late. The sisters had allowed themselves to be lulled by the joy of homecoming and then of watching a child grow. They had forgotten about Kitty's gift, it seemed, but now they had to do something.

She had to do something. It was up to her, as usual, to clean up Kitty's mess.

Thekla made her announcement in the kitchen, where the sisters had gathered for brunch.

"The child is getting older. We must clear the house."

The kitchens were to be locked when not in use and every mirror removed from the property.

The sisters were shocked. Their faces aligned like moons around an angry planet. This idea seemed to come out of nowhere and they could not seem to fathom that Thekla would go to such drastic lengths.

Ingeburg shook her head. "This is absurd, Thekla. You know perfectly well there is no way to prevent Kitty's gift from manifesting. Nothing we do will make a difference. Nothing. I do not understand why we must engage in such futility."

"She is right, you know. Thekla, you must realize how senseless this is. Will we shave the jagged bark from every tree? Lock her in her room? We cannot keep her prisoner here forever." Eva's eyes were wide with concern.

Thekla could not help herself. She was driven by fear, but pride had an even louder voice. She would not let Kitty win this battle. She resented her sister and the way she so smugly played with their lives, doing whatever she so desired and at whatever whim.

No, Kitty would not have her way in this, no matter the cost.

"I hear you, sisters, but I have decided. Tomorrow the mirrors come down. We must take no chances."

It was only the beginning; Thekla had not revealed the full shape of her plan. Her sisters did not know how devious Kitty could be, but Thekla remembered. Helena's questions had brought it all back in awful detail.

It had happened just after their brother died. Katza had hid in her room, coming out only to eat, but even then she'd been a pale shade at the table, hardly tasting her food.

Thekla had felt sorry for her sister and had attempted to fold Katza under her small, protective wing. Katza had been as unresponsive as their father, though she had no illness to blame. They had all watched Papa decay into depression. All of his aspirations were dead with Louis, his firstborn and only son, and there was no Dream King to lead him out of the dark.

After a time, Thekla had given up on Katza. There had

still been the smaller sisters to tend and Thekla had felt it her duty to help her mother see to their needs. It had been a great burden for such a young girl, but she had taken it on willingly because she knew no one else was able. And she still had the joy of her music to balance the weight.

She had allowed herself no time to grieve for her brother. There were moments, most often in the kitchen, when she'd thought she'd seen him stride in—rifle over his shoulder and a smile on his face—and she felt her own smile begin to form in return. And then the vision would fade, and she'd remember: Louis was gone—not gone like Katza, who was still there but not present, but well and truly gone to a place none could follow. Thekla had been lonely, and in her loneliness, had begun to talk to Louis' ghost.

"Why did you leave?" she had asked him one day as he appeared at dawn.

Thekla had been standing at her bedroom window to watch the sun rise, to capture a moment of quiet before the house began to stir. She had not been sleeping well, the nightmares were growing worse by the week, and she was always worried about any number of things that could go wrong in the day.

Louis had not answered. Instead, as the sun had risen slightly higher and the patterns of shadow shifted on the floor, he had faded into light.

"I miss you," she'd said another time, out in the gardens where she thought she saw him standing by a tree. The shade had smiled, glanced at the upper rooms of the house, and then vanished.

She had believed she'd seen a message in that glance and so she had dared, at last, to knock again on Katza's door.

There had been a voice from beyond the thick wood, muffled and barely audible. "Who is it?"

"It is Thekla. Please let me in."

A few moments had passed in which Thekla had fidgeted, afraid of what she would see beyond the door. It had opened slowly to reveal Katza, her once neatly wound braid hanging in unkempt tangles past her shoulders, her dress rumpled and no shoes on her feet.

Thekla had observed these things but had not said a word about them.

Katza had taken her by the shoulder and pulled her into the darkened room. The curtains had been drawn; it could have been night and no one would have known the difference. She had shut the door behind them and led Thekla to the bed, where Katza sat with her head in her hands.

"Katza? I'm worried about you. So is Louis."

Katza had looked sharply at her sister. "What are you talking about?"

Thekla had lowered her eyes. She did not want to share this secret with her sister. It was all she had of Louis; she wanted to keep it for herself. But Katza was so miserable, Thekla had thought. Maybe it would help.

"I see him, sometimes."

"Come here," Katza had said as she reached out her arms.

Thekla had fallen into them with an aching relief.

"You have taken on so many of the responsibilities of this house. I have neglected you. Will you forgive me?"

Thekla had sniffled and wrapped her arms more tightly around Katza's waist. "Yes."

"Hush now. There is too much sadness here already. We've got to get out, you and I. Will you leave with me?"

At that moment, Thekla would have done anything her sister suggested, so grateful was she to have been noticed by her again. She had nodded and wiped her eyes with a sleeve.

"Good. We must act as though nothing has changed. I am making plans now. Give me a little more time, my sister, and then we will go."

"But what of the others?" Thekla could not forget them.

"They will be fine. Mama is here, she will soon come to her senses, and there are plenty of other people to tend to them in the meantime. You'll make yourself sick worrying so. Please?"

Thekla had nodded again, trusting in Katza's wisdom, and had not complained when Katza ushered her out of the room with a finger to her lips.

"Don't say a word to anyone. This is our secret."

Thekla had done as Katza instructed. She'd left her sisters to the care of their tutors and nannies and let music command her attention as it had always done. Soon enough, Mama had turned her own attention back to her children, even smiling at Eva's babble now and again. Thekla had known then that all would be well. She had relaxed and waited, and stifled her confusion when Katza made silent appearances at the table.

The day after their father's funeral, Katza had not appeared for breakfast.

"Thekla, would you please go ask your sister if she

is coming down this morning?" Mama had not seemed concerned.

Thekla had crept up to Katza's room and knocked on the heavy door. She'd waited; there'd been no answer. She'd knocked again, but something had told her that Katza was not there. She'd opened the door and let the light from the hall slowly enter the room. It had been dark and empty, the bed strewn with discarded clothes. Katza was gone.

Thekla had stood as still as a mouse does in those few moments when it must decide if the thing that has caught its attention is dangerous. That Katza had left without her did not sink in right away. Thekla had walked slowly toward the windows and drawn the curtains aside. Their plush fabric had swung open to reveal an expanse of green, the very lawn on which she, Katza, and Louis had shared a picnic on Katza's last birthday. Thekla had imagined she'd seen them, hand in hand, running away from the house.

She had not cried. Instead, she had turned back toward the empty room, noticed the way motes of dust sparkled in the sun and the gleam of burnished wood on the four-poster bed. The room had already assumed the qualities of a museum; all had been quiet except for the sound of Thekla breathing as she looked over the relics of her sister's life, left behind. As was she. It had been her own fault for believing in Katza. Thekla had promised herself she would never weaken again.

Her sisters were unaware of Thekla's heartbreak. Thekla had never mentioned that she'd known of Katza's intentions, or that she had agreed to leave with her. That was Thekla's cross to bear. She stiffened her shoulders accordingly. She came from a strong line of women, and it was their strength she drew upon now. First, the mirrors. *And then*, she thought, *the rest of it*. She would hear no argument from any.

Chapter 10

HELENA STOOD IN A PRETTY WHITE FROCK WITH HER FINGERS in her mouth, a habit she kept though her aunts disapproved. "Hope," she said, her words garbled. "Make them stop."

Hope took Helena by the hand and pulled her into the hall. The workmen had already been and gone there and on the wall a large, clean square stood out like a lost bit of patchwork.

"Why are they taking away all of our mirrors?" Helena stamped her foot on the floor.

Hope fingered the keys at her belt. There was now a sturdy lock on the kitchen door, as though Helena was in some kind of danger from the cutlery. Mirrors, some hundreds of years old, were being removed from the walls of each room and hall in the house. Even Elfrieda's precious silver-handled mirror had been collected and thrown into a bag with some others. The sisters were in shock, but Hope wasn't allowed time to react. She had to keep Helena out of the way and Helena was having none of it.

Hope wanted to tell Helena the truth. She wanted to say, *she only means to protect you*, but that would unleash too many more questions and Hope could not answer them all. Kitty's spell rustled in the corner. It was not Hope's place to speak with Helena about her unusual gifts. Let her live on in the comfort of ignorance for as long as she was able.

It would be better for her, Hope surmised, to discover the truth on her own.

"I don't know. We'll have to ask Aunt Thekla after they've gone. She is busy now."

"Aunt Thekla probably did this."

Helena tried to lure Hope into speaking the truth with her eyes, but Hope was on to her little tricks and manipulations. Helena might work her own brand of magic on her aunts, but Hope was completely immune.

"Then you'll just have to ask her yourself," Hope said. She led Helena unwillingly into the kitchen, where there weren't any mirrors to miss.

"Would you like a glass of milk?" Hope thought to appease Helena before she began to howl.

"Yes," Helena said and held out her hand.

Hope guessed that Helena had mentioned the bird to Thekla and that this was the result. It was madness—Thekla feared the glass in the mirrors, but they were surely not the only things that might cause Helena harm. There were splinters in the old wood, thorns in the garden, and glass lamps all over the house. Would they vanish next? There was certainly more to come.

Hope had to admit that Thekla was right about one thing. They had grown too complacent, their attention focused on Helena's evident gifts while the other had been all but forgotten. Hope was just as much to blame as any of them, but none knew exactly what they should watch for. Kitty had done nothing since their return, had not once shown her face, but that meant nothing. The deed had been done and Kitty was no doubt waiting, like the rest of them, for her gift to be opened. Hope glanced at Helena and heard again the sound of her foot coming down on the flagstones. Perhaps it already had.

She wondered what Helena was thinking as she sat so calmly and sipped at her milk. The house was full of strange faces; Helena lived a secluded life and saw no one but those approved by Thekla to enter. Tutors, the doctor, her aunts: all deferred to Helena. These men hardly saw her as they passed by in the hall.

Hope wasn't blind; she could see how Helena ruled everyone who entered her circle. Helena should be screaming at this intrusion and the upheaval it was causing. Instead, she sat with her head down and said nothing.

They listened for a while to the bustle in the house until Helena finally asked, "What will we do without the mirrors, Hope?"

The sound of her voice, delicate and soft in this rare moment of confusion, drew Hope's sympathy.

"We will learn to live without them, Helena. Would you like an apple?" she asked as she reached for one from the table. "I will peel it for you."

She turned and Hope thought her heart would break at the sight of Helena's face. Her eyes begged for a truth Hope could not give her. Instead, Hope took her into her arms. To Hope's surprise, Helena did not pull away.

It lasted for only a moment. Helena stiffened and turned

back into stone and Hope left her to sulking. There was laundry to fold and hems to mend and supper to think about and the day had been thrown into chaos.

Hope scoffed at the lock on the pantry door and then realized it might be the only good thing to come of Thekla's decision. There were objects she kept inside that were not meant for others to find. She sorted through her keys until she found the right one. This will take some getting used to, she thought as it turned in the lock. The pantry was her pride; it was a long room stocked with goods and linens and one wall was lined with drawers. She stepped inside and pulled one open and took out a small leather pouch. It was warm in her palm; she kissed it and tucked it into her pocket.

"Hope?"

Helena's voice called her out of the pantry—Hope carefully locked the door as it closed behind her. "What is it, Helena?"

"Take me into the garden."

Death had raised its famished head.

CHAPTER 11

EVERYONE WAS HUMBLED BY THE REMOVAL OF THE MIRRORS, even Thekla, who'd ordered it done. The twins were unusually quiet. Zilli and Elfrieda stayed in their rooms. Ingeburg stalked through the naked halls and decried a life without reflection. Eva sat in the kitchen, day after day, the heavy key on a loop at her belt a constant reminder of Kitty's gift. Gone were the days when the sisters could gather at mealtimes, or to share the bounty of the gardens with Hope, without thought of locking and unlocking doors. Even Hope's good nature had been affected by Thekla's decision. She could often be found behind the sealed doors staring into her pots and pans, as though scrying in their copper depths for a brighter future.

Eva was at a loss. The empty walls of the house towered around her no matter where she went. Their flat and barren surfaces seemed to beg for decoration, but the sisters were forbidden to hang anything else upon them. It was awful, but what the lack represented for Eva was worse. She could not come to terms with her sister's drastic measures and felt like a traitor for it.

She owed her good life to Thekla—they all did. Her sister had kept the family together and raised them when Mama had died, on her own and with no help from anyone. Thekla had never once led them astray. She knew best and they all believed it, but what if they were wrong? It was difficult to imagine going against Thekla in any matter, yet Eva did imagine it.

They knew nothing of Kitty, not really. The more Eva questioned it, the more she realized that they had each formed an opinion of Kitty by way of Thekla. Whoever Thekla loved, they loved. Whoever Thekla despised, they despised. A surge of guilt flooded Eva as these ideas took shape, as though she was already defying her sister just by considering them. She fussed with a button on her sweater. The pearl slipped through her fingers, too small to grasp.

Eva decided, after a great deal of sighing and mumbling, to visit Kitty herself. She would form her own opinion, once and for all.

It was treachery. Eva left through the kitchen while Thekla was busy elsewhere. She felt like a thief as she crept through the gardens, hoping to avoid detection. Eva did not remember much of Kitty beyond her appearance at Helena's christening. She recalled a young face, long hair kept in a neat braid, and heard laughter, but when she tried to get a sense of the person, there was only an empty space. When Kitty left it was as though a piece of the family puzzle went missing beneath the rug. Eva got used to the missing piece, as people will, and filled in the hole with her own ideas about whoever once fit there. Thekla's ideas, she reminded herself.

As the years had passed, the legend of Kitty had grown. Demented, cursed, wild: these were the words used to describe their sister, spoken so often their true meanings had become dulled. Was Kitty demented? She had not seemed so at the christening. Indecipherable, yes, but not mad—at least no more so than Thekla, who had brought the mirrors down.

When Eva reached the door to the coach house, she found it already open. She cursed under her breath. She did not need a reminder of Kitty's extra gift, not when she was trying to see her sister in a different light. Without warning, Kitty appeared in the doorway. Eva felt a blush darken her cheeks. She put her hand to her face before she realized what she was doing.

"You were expecting me."

"Of course I was." Kitty smiled and held the door open, ushering Eva inside.

It was no way to begin the encounter. Eva was flustered, her stomach rumbled and Kitty, her blue eyes as clear as still water, seemed more like a cat intent on a mouse than an old woman in a floral housedress.

I defied Kitty once, Eva remembered. Kitty might still hold it against her.

"Make yourself comfortable," Kitty waved at the cluster of chairs that filled the sitting room at the front of the small, weathered coach house.

Eva doubted she would find comfort anywhere in Kitty's presence, but she eased herself into a cushioned armchair and watched her eldest sister do the same. Beneath the wrinkles and the stray white hairs that fell away from her bun, Eva found a familiar echo of Kitty's youth. Eva was shocked at the bond she felt; it was almost as though they had never been apart. They could easily have embraced, but did not.

Eva was unsure of how to begin, or even what the

conversation should be about. She simply wanted to get a sense of her sister and try to understand how things had come to such a pass.

"Katza," Eva used her formal name. "How have you been?"

"I've been well, thank you for asking, though I doubt you came here to check on the state of my health." Kitty saw no need for pleasantries between them.

Karl startled Eva when he entered the room, bearing a tray of coffee and marzipan sweets. She blinked, stunned to find a man in her sister's household. Her surprise quickly faded to gratitude for the distraction. Eva needed a moment to consider Kitty's blunt words. She watched in horror as Kitty took three of the round candies and popped them into her mouth like a greedy child.

"Do have one." She lifted the tray towards Eva. "From München. Very tasty," she said between bites.

Eva took one delicately between thumb and forefinger. It was delicious, but she did not have another. She was not very fond of sweets.

"Suit yourself," Kitty said.

"Precisely."

Kitty stopped chewing and inspected her sister, caught the look of determination on her face. *This might be interesting.* Kitty swallowed.

"Karl, throw another log on that fire, will you? I feel a draft." Kitty turned her head in order to better hear Eva.

Karl, his expression one of intense disinterest, did as she asked. As soon as he finished and left the room, Eva spoke.

"I won't waste your time, Katza. All of my life I have

followed in Thekla's footsteps. I have allowed her to form my opinions for me—I suspect we all have. We had no one else." She stopped; she was not here to cast blame. "It occurs to me that I don't really know you, and I'd like to."

Kitty shifted in her seat, moving her bulky thighs to a more comfortable position in the chair. It had seen better days, as had she. She was as unsettled by Eva's candor as Eva had been by her own.

"There's not much to know, Eva. I am an old woman, like yourself, who has carved out a small life by trial and error."

"But why have you carved that life out alone? Why did you go off on your own, seclude yourself from us and leave us as you did? I think you owe us the truth."

Kitty shuffled in her seat, her face revealing nothing. "You are correct, Eva. There are many things you do not know about this family, and you are better off for it. Thekla did her very best by you all, be sure of it. Even had I stayed, she would have mothered you no differently."

"But you didn't stay and the family has been divided ever since. Did you know that Mama used to cry at nights for you? You couldn't even bring yourself to attend her funeral. There must be something to this, and I intend to find out what it is."

Eva sat back and took a sip of coffee, still steaming in the cup. She noticed the pattern, an old Schumann floral, and silently complimented Kitty on her taste.

"You always were a determined child." Kitty said.

"How would you know?" Eva set her cup down gently, though she would rather smash it to bits. Her anger surprised her, but now was no time to unleash it.

"What has Thekla done to put you in this state?" Kitty waved her hand in dismissal. "No, I know it must be something. I may not know much of you, as you suggest, but I do know Thekla. Tell me what it is and I will answer your question."

It seemed like a fair bargain. It couldn't hurt *(could it?)* to tell Kitty about the mirrors. It was her gift to Helena that was causing all the fuss in the first place.

"She has had every mirror removed from the house and I'm afraid it is only the beginning. She is obsessed with protecting Helena from your gift, so much so that I fear she will do more harm than good. You cannot really mean for the girl to die."

Kitty shifted in her chair again. "If she finds out you've been here, she will have a fit."

"I know. I have no intention of telling her. What we say between us remains between us. I simply must have some answers. I cannot live under her new regime without some insight as to why she hates you so."

"You are right to think that Thekla hates me. I am sure she does." Kitty took a breath. "Before I left home, I allowed Thekla to believe that we would be going together."

Kitty paused again. "I imagine she was very hurt when I did not take her with me."

Eva was floored. How could Kitty have been so cruel? There was more truth to the matter of Kitty's wicked ways than she'd suspected.

"Do not judge me too harshly. Wouldn't you like to know why I acted as I did?"

Since Kitty was talking, Eva decided to listen. She raised

her chin, giving the slightest indication that Kitty should continue.

"We all had a very difficult time after Louis died."

Kitty paused for moment and closed her eyes, as though searching for the strength to continue there behind her lids.

"Thekla, I think now, had the hardest time of it, though she brought most of it on herself. She was wearing herself ragged taking care of you all. She was only eleven years old and I feared for her health. I suggested she might leave with me to distract her from her self-imposed duties. It worked, if only for a time."

"And then you left without her. What did you think that would do to her?"

Eva could not imagine how betrayed Thekla must have felt, but she was beginning to understand why her sister had held her grudge against Kitty for all of these many years. She would have, too.

"I don't know. I was selfish—yes, I admit it. I could not stay there any longer."

"Well, that certainly explains some things. I can't say I approve, but I do appreciate your honesty. However," Eva cleared her throat, "you've still not answered all of my questions. Do you intend for your gift to harm Helena?"

Kitty gazed at the window and out of it, lost for a moment in her thoughts.

"Leave it to Thekla to take my gift at face value and then blow it out of proportion. I can assure you," Kitty said, "that my gift will not harm the child."

It was all she would say.

Eva, sensing the conversation was over, rose to her feet. Kitty nodded her goodbye as Karl showed Eva to the door.

Eva, on the step, watched it close behind her. The latch clicked, the birds perched on the porch began singing and the sun came out from behind a cloud. These things fell into Eva—an end and a beginning. It was a new era for them all.

₧₧

Kitty had seen her sister coming, but had got no sense of what the visit would be about. Eva was not, of course, the toddler Kitty remembered. She'd felt like a mouse, trapped by a cat with one swipe of her paw. Kitty flinched and rubbed her hands together as her knuckles pressed through her skin like little rusted knives. The old familiar ache was creeping through her thighs and her vision blurred with pain. Kitty had missed all of the years that had made Eva the woman who'd sat across from her, waiting for an answer. Kitty had been willing to have the conversation, if only to give Eva a measure of peace, but there were places she still would not go, not even if asked. Kitty had to bear this burden alone.

Kitty did not dream that night. Her sleep was filled with memory, flashes like in a picture show, still-lifes flickering one by one in front of her vision. A moment of Louis and then Magdalena, there Eva as a child, there Papa before his demise, his black coat still neatly pressed, even though sorrow had him all wrinkled up.

If she could go back far enough, she would topple a tree on that golden sleigh, tear Ludwig from the seat and leave him lying in the drifts of snow that had piled beneath the window. She would have listened for his knock and answered the door, told him to be on his way. No matter that he was king or mad—she did not care. She would do anything to keep that night from happening. Why had the blizzard ever blown him in?

He would have snared her brother anyway, she reasoned in her half-stupor, as consciousness crept over her and then slid off again. It was not that night, but another, far fouler night, that she must prevent. As sleep began to claim her, she saw Louis' lifeless face hanging just beneath the surface of the lake.

CHAPTER 12

THEKLA'S DESIGN BECAME CLEAR AS TIME WENT ON. AFTER the mirrors and the locks on the doors, she had every sharp object in the house removed, except for those needed by Hope to manage her cooking. When they took Helena's favorite music box away because of its sharp brass corners, Helena tore down the hallway curtains in her outrage. Even that did not stop Thekla. She would do anything to keep Helena safe from Kitty's gift, she said, and everyone soon realized she meant it.

It was a slow progression. Some days the sisters woke to find carpenters in the back hall, sanding and painting the woodwork. Other times men appeared on the roof, nailing down slate or removing it, and once Thekla even had a crew rip out the roses. The thorns, she said, posed a hazard to Helena. The roses, unconcerned, reappeared the very next day. Each year brought a new surprise, another change, another bit of their home remade anew, or *modernized*, as Thekla liked to say.

Eva was not fooled. She knew what drove Thekla, but also knew that Kitty hadn't told the entire tale those few years ago. Kitty had said it herself—Eva was better off not knowing the whole truth. Eva doubted that, but a confrontation with Thekla would not end well and Kitty had said all she would. Eva had always believed that it was Louis' death that had severed the family, but she found herself wondering if something else might have cut even more deeply into their roots. All roads led to Louis, but he was dead.

Only the sisters survived, and they now lived in fear. Its cold blanket wrapped around their shoulders and the routines they had established as a family were all but gone. Thekla was distant, the others grouped in twos and threes and the bonds between them all were quietly fraying.

Everything was connected, somehow. If Eva could piece it all together, she would be able to stop Thekla from bringing the whole house down around their heads. Thekla seemed precariously close to madness, and these crazy schemes of hers could not be good for the child. The house had been stripped of anything useful; it was more like a prison than a home, all for a gift none understood in the first place. That was it—they were guessing at Kitty's intent, even Thekla. Especially Thekla, though she did have good reason to suspect the worst. Helena would certainly bear watching. None of this would be happening if it were not for her gift. Maybe it was she who held the key.

None of them had what Eva would call a close relationship with their prodigy. Helena, at eleven years of age, was perfection itself. She could also be perfectly nasty. She was gorgeous and graceful, intelligent and exquisitely talented, but the sisters were not so proud of their creation these days.

They never spoke out loud of it, but one of them should have thought to give Helena kindness, or love, or at least a little bit of compassion. As far as Eva could tell, she had none. Perhaps eight had been too many gifts; they crowded out everything else. They all agreed that Helena was precisely what they had made her. Not one drop of anything else had grown within her.

It could be that Helena was the only one who would ever know the truth of Kitty's gift, but by then it might be too late. The best Eva had done was to trade death for sleep, and even she did not know what that might really mean.

Sleep rather than death? If and when Helena woke, she might still die the moment her eyes opened. It was a horrible thought and one Eva did not want to follow, though she was sure there was something at its end. It was a muddle and high time, Eva felt, to take matters into her own hands.

Eva found Hope, as usual, in the kitchen. Hope was preparing a batch of fresh bread and had flour up to her elbows.

"Do you ever leave this room?" Eva teased her as she wiped crumbs from the cutting board into the sink. She liked to help in the kitchen, though Hope often chased her away.

Hope was always the same, no matter how anything changed. Eva looked at their old housekeeper, saw hair as grey as her own, the neat apron tied around her thick waist and her stoic expression, intent on the bread.

"Hope, you spend a lot of time with Helena." Easy, she thought. Let's not say too much. "Have you noticed anything unusual about her?"

"Unusual?" Hope chuckled.

"You know what I mean," Eva said, perhaps too sharply.

Hope pounded the dough. "No, I can't say that I have."

"Are you certain? There is no need to keep the truth from me." Eva prodded a little harder.

"She does ask a lot of questions." Hope shrugged and carried on.

Hope acted as though this was any other conversation and perhaps, for her, it was. Eva grew silent, fiddled with the dishcloth and absentmindedly wiped the counter.

Hope was right. Helena did ask a lot of questions, and she would ask many more as time went on. She would dig the truth out of one of them; they had given her a stunning intellect for that very purpose. Perhaps they should have considered the full implications. One day Helena was sure to outwit her own makers. What would they do then?

☙ ❧

As Eva left the kitchen, Hope shook her head at the sorry state of things. Her strong hands kneaded the dough, patted it out in a baker's rhythm known only to those who work their own bread. She knew all too well of Helena's unusual behavior.

Hope knew the rules: do your job and stay out of their business and keep them out of yours. But Thekla had made the family Hope's business soon after they'd hired her. Thekla had pulled her aside and offered a generous bargain. In exchange for a lifetime of security, she asked only that

Hope be loyal to them and any they took in. It had been an easy agreement to make, for Hope was already fond of the sisters. She had grown to love Lena, and now she loved Helena as well.

The family had more sense than this. Thekla grew more agitated by the hour. Eva was a bundle of nerves and the others simply seemed fragile and, for the first time, old. Helena was a beautiful girl, but beneath that fine exterior a monster lurked unseen by any but Hope, who watched it come out in the garden every now and then. The last time it had been a kitten that had strayed into Helena's hands. She had stroked its ears and kissed its nose and then she had snapped its neck. Hope still did not know why Helena did these terrible things, but her suspicions remained unchanged.

Quietly cruel, as though cruelty had no part in it, Helena gave no thought to the pain she caused in others. It was not in her to contemplate such things; this was something every one of them knew. Hope did not hold it against Helena, but she did want to better understand the girl so she could better provide for her needs. Eva must want something, too. But what? She'd never seen Helena's ugliest side and in any case, it was not something Hope would share.

Hope continued to work the dough until it was soft and pliant, and then scooped it into a bowl and left it to rise. She washed her hands meticulously and dried them on the towel. In the pantry, she opened one of the drawers. Hope took out the pouch, a small square of leather tied up with a silken cord. She'd been working on it for years.

Helena did as she pleased despite the consequences, as

though she had no concept of cause and effect, and Hope believed she knew why. She recalled Kitty's words clearly, as did they all. Everyone feared for Helena, the innocent child, the victim of Kitty's curse. They thought it was Helena's death that Kitty wanted. After what Hope had seen, she couldn't help but wonder. Hope put the pieces together as best as she was able and came to an awful conclusion. Kitty had created in Helena a monster, a killer with no remorse. Kitty did mean for someone to die, it seemed, but Helena was merely her weapon.

Hope frowned. None of the sisters—not even Kitty—knew Hope had weapons of her own.

Hope's magic was of simple things. A woven thread, a thimble, stone, a snippet of hair, and a drop of earth for good measure were the tools of her trade. She'd learned it well and loyalty had everything to do with it. Hope looked at her arms, thick and strong from years of housework: wringing laundry by hand, peeling potatoes, rolling dough. Hope knew her place and was firmly planted in it.

She did more than fold the sisters' sheets that night. By the light of a waning moon she wove her spell.

Sometimes, no matter how well we lay them, our plans fall apart because some chance thing occurs. Hope called these nuisances the spiders of fate and she was going to catch one. Try as they might, the sisters would never stop Kitty's gift from flowering. Helena, on the other hand, could outsmart Frau Holle herself. Hope saw ahead of them just such an instance approaching, where Helena's wit might be all that saved the day.

Yes, Hope mused, Helena was gifted, but there are times

when even a prodigy needs a little help. There was no guarantee that Hope could do it, but she had to take the chance. One spider caught in the net, that was all Hope needed, and Kitty's plan could fall apart. Hope had already seen the very spider she needed, crawling about in the pantry. She laid her trap, bit by bit, as the household carried on.

CHAPTER 13

"NOT THE WINDOWS, THEKLA. YOU CANNOT BE SERIOUS!"
Ingeburg stood in the hall with her hands on her hips, nose
to nose with Thekla. Eva came down the steps to find them
arguing. It was an unprecedented sight.

"I am serious."

"Excuse me, I couldn't help but overhear you."

Eva nudged her way in between the two women, using her
new cane as leverage. It was quite a nice piece, made from
stout local wood and carved all over with vines. She was
initially ashamed of her need for it, but it would serve well,
she now decided, in cases such as this.

"What are you doing with the windows?" she asked once
she'd planted herself between them.

"I am having them boarded up." Thekla looked down her
nose at Eva, daring her to argue.

"She means it." Ingeburg almost stamped her foot in fury.
"She actually means it."

"I see that. Board them up? Thekla, you don't expect
us to agree to this, do you?" Eva's stomach churned at the
thought.

"Helena will be sixteen years old in less than a week. We are still unprepared. Kitty's curse could strike at any time! These windows are a danger. They cannot be allowed to remain."

Eva gaped.

"There must over two hundred of them! You'll turn the place into a tomb."

"Precisely. That is over two hundred opportunities for Kitty's curse to manifest. It will not be a tomb. For heaven's sake, Eva, we have lamps."

"These windows are older than we are. You will only damage the house and increase all of our chances of injury with the destruction. And no, we do not have lamps. You had them removed three years ago. We have *fixtures*." The sarcasm in her voice was unmistakable, but Eva had to say it. She felt as though she was on fire and about to explode.

"Listen to the voice of reason, will you?" Ingeburg implored.

"Please, Thekla. Let us at least discuss this before you make any decisions. Something of this magnitude involves us all." Eva had feared it would come to this. "We will have a family meeting, tonight if you like, after Helena has gone to sleep."

Thekla capitulated. It was beneath her to stand in the hallway and argue with anyone.

"Tonight then. Ten o'clock. Sharp."

Thekla turned her back to her sisters and scuttled away, leaning heavily on her cane.

Eva and Ingeburg exchanged a glance, but held their silence until the sound of Thekla's footsteps faded.

"Do you think she will do it?" Ingeburg said, trembling.

"Yes, I'm afraid I do. Let us not stand here and discuss this, however. Come with me." Eva led Ingeburg up the stairs and locked her bedroom door behind them.

"Are you sure this secrecy is necessary?"

"I am." Eva felt as though she'd been thrown into an old detective film. She straightened her back. She was about to do something incredible. "Please, sit down."

In the corner of the room, two chairs and a table were arranged by an east-facing window. Eva's bedroom was right beside Thekla's, in the northeastern corner of the house, where the open hall met the long, north wing. Her view included a bit of the lake, but it did not disturb her. It made her feel closer to Louis, somehow, though she did not remember him. The lake was calm today, and on it two boats drifted without direction. Eva wished she had time to relax and enjoy the scene.

"Be truthful with me, Ingeburg. Don't you find our sister's behavior somewhat disturbing?" It was the first time she'd mentioned her concerns to any of her sisters. Eva wasn't certain of how Ingeburg would answer, but the days of sheepishly living with Thekla's decisions were gone.

"Of course I do. I've tolerated her episodes even though most have annoyed me, but only because she had Helena's best interests at heart. I am no longer convinced that is the case, but I've no idea what to do about it." Ingeburg flinched as the words left her mouth.

"Leave that to me," Eva said.

Ingeburg raised an eyebrow. "What can you do?"

"I am going to speak with Kitty."

"You what?" Ingeburg was suffering shock after shock,

and it seemed this one would be her undoing. She put her hand to her heart, as though to determine whether or not it was still beating.

"Oh for heaven's sake," Eva said. "Calm down. It won't be the first time. I tell you, there is a deeper divide between them than we ever imagined. Thekla has gone far beyond an attempt to protect Helena. She is out to prove something to Kitty and won't stop until she's done it."

"What do you mean?" Ingeburg was astounded by her sister's bravery.

Eva told Ingeburg the story of how Kitty had left Thekla after the death of Louis. She did not have to mention how heartbreaking it must have been to young Thekla—Ingeburg knew. She grasped Eva's hand in sympathy as tears began to form in their eyes.

"It's no wonder Thekla feels like she does, but that is still no excuse to wreck the place." Ingeburg stopped, struck by a thought. "Have you asked Kitty about her gift?" Would Eva dare?

"Yes, as a matter of fact, I have. She insists her gift will not harm Helena. But I tell you, I'm not sure I believe her."

"I certainly don't believe it. How can her gift not be harmful? What nonsense is she speaking?"

"She seems to believe herself, and she should know."

"But she could have been lying."

"I agree, but I don't think she was. It isn't her words I don't trust. I honestly think she believes what she is saying. I also think her definition of *harm* may not be ours."

"Even if she is being truthful, how can she help us now?"

"I'm not certain," Eva said, "but she must. She is part of this family, too. You let our sisters know of tonight's meeting. Thekla won't have her way in this. Trust me."

The two sisters parted. Ingeburg went off to find the others while Eva took the old garden path. The lock Thekla had put on the door leading out to the courtyard had rusted, and only opened after being given a good thwack with Eva's cane.

Kitty answered her door with a smile. Eva was prepared this time; she returned Kitty's bright welcome with one of her own as she stepped under the lintel. Eva did not waste her words.

"I'm concerned about recent developments. Thekla's latest idea seems a bit," Eva hesitated, unsure of how much to reveal, "extravagant. You must help me stop her."

She'd done it. Thekla was completely betrayed.

"Don't you mean Thekla's latest fit?" Kitty waved her hand at Eva as if to say *no matter, you do not have to agree.* "I already know. I am aware of how seriously Thekla takes matters. I've told you once before and I am telling you again. Helena is safe."

"Thekla will never believe that. You say no harm will come to Helena by way of your gift, but from where I am standing, it looks as though it already has. Helena is a willful young woman. What Thekla has planned can only bring trouble to us all."

"What do you mean by willful?" Kitty leaned forward in her chair and watched her sister shuffle her feet and pluck at some lint on her sweater.

"I mean," Eva leaned forward, "if Helena disagrees with

Thekla's actions, she's liable to burn the house down around us. It wouldn't surprise me if she took all of the grounds with it." She could not hide the truth, not any longer.

"I see," Kitty said, and she did. "She's bound to have her flaws, the way you all treat her."

"That's not the point." Eva would not take the bait. "Assuring me your gift will not harm Helena is not enough. You must tell me what you meant by it, or I'll never change Thekla's mind."

"Oh come now, Eva. Nothing you say about me or my gift will move Thekla in any way. Listen." Kitty sat up and straightened her shoulders. "You do remember my gift, don't you? Think now. What did I say?"

Eva heard the words clearly: *Death shall lead you back.*

Kitty sat in the lengthening silence until Eva suddenly clenched her hands.

I have been such a fool, Eva thought.

Kitty had never specified whose death she had in mind. But if it wasn't Helena—who? It could be any one of them, or none. It was a strange game of roulette Kitty played and it thrilled Eva to think they were equally at her mercy.

Thekla knows how the gifts work, too, Eva thought, and felt a wave of compassion roll over her for her sister. Thekla feared for Helena, yes, but also for all of them and her fear had overwhelmed her reason. Thekla had spent a lifetime caring for her sisters. There was no way she would stop now. Eva came to a radical and sudden conclusion: Helena's gift had to manifest. It was the only way to end a life of tyranny and fear.

CHAPTER 14

EVA RETURNED TO THE HOUSE AND FOUND HELENA EASILY—
the Latin tutor was striding furiously down the hall toward
the wide, front doors.

"I cannot do this another minute!" he shouted as he
hurried past Eva, his lapels flapping and a half-eaten book in
his hands.

Let Thekla handle it, Eva thought. Thekla enjoyed this kind
of thing. Eva turned as Helena glided out of the library with a
wicked smile on her face. Eva ignored the scene, for it would
only repeat next week with a different victim.

Helena had become a glacial young woman, as heartless
as the ice that formed on the eaves in winter. Eva and her
sisters stepped lightly around Helena's temper. It was hard to
detect; her rages never seemed to originate in any anger. Hers
was a calculated fury, which made it all the more frightening,
yet Helena could also be the most pleasant company possible.
She was undeniably stunning and when she smiled, it was as
though the sun shone just for them.

The sisters did their best to protect her, but none of them
were as imaginative as Thekla about what that protection
entailed. Eva was about to throw it all to the wind, but that

didn't trouble her nearly as much as did the idea of talking with Helena. If she said the wrong thing, or showed any hesitation, Helena would have her for dinner. Eva had to act now, before her courage failed her.

"Helena," Eva said as Helena walked by, "would you care to explore the house with me?"

Helena stopped abruptly. Her face revealed nothing. "Yes, Aunt Eva, I would like that."

Eva withheld a breath of relief and assumed the role of a blundering, helpless old lady. It was always best to let Helena feel in control.

"Good girl. Take my hand, I'm not as young as I look."

Helena allowed Eva to lead her up the stairs. At the end of the south wing, Eva pulled a key from her pocket and unlocked the door to the third floor. Helena watched intently, but did not say a word as they climbed a second set of stairs.

Like the lower floors, the third had been refurbished before they arrived and then dismantled during one of Thekla's crusades. The door had been locked and, as far as Eva knew, no one had gone up there since. None of the sisters inhabited any of the rooms and the floorboards were covered in dust. They could certainly have used the space, but their knees weren't up to the task of climbing two sets of stairs. One was more than enough, as Eva's legs soon reminded her.

At the third floor landing, Eva had to rest. She let go of Helena's hand and nodded for her to go off and explore. "Give me but a moment, and then come right back. We are going into the attics."

Eva watched Helena turn toward a door hanging ajar at the

end of the hallway. Helena pushed it open; there was nothing to see but a four-poster bed, a white sheet hung over it to keep the wood free of dust. Eva smiled as Helena waved a cobweb away from her face.

"Come now," Eva called as she hobbled in the opposite direction. She stopped before a long swath of wall.

"One more set of stairs," Eva said as she inserted a key into a hole hidden at eye-level among the design in the paper. A door swung silently outwards. They made their way slowly up the final, narrow stair. Helena kept pace behind her aunt, who grappled with the railing with one hand and flailed for the light with her other. There was a click as Eva pulled a chain; a bulb flared on overhead.

"Here we are," Eva said as she hauled herself up the last step.

The room spread out on each side of her, a huge expanse of space cluttered with all of those things one would expect to find in an old home's attic, musty and stinking of mice. Helena sneezed.

"It's filthy."

The floor beneath Helena's feet was free of dust, but in the far corners of the room, where light hardly reached, motes flew in the rafters thick as fog.

"What is this mess?" she asked.

"Furniture, old clothes—you never know. Most of this was probably here when I was a child, and that was many years ago. This room holds what is left of the family's past."

"Why hasn't Aunt Thekla cleaned it out?"

Eva glanced sharply at Helena, who never spoke of the

strange doings in the household. "I imagine she does not remember these things are here."

Eva hadn't known there was an attic—it was Hope who found the key and then the door. Eva had come up several times since and stood in the light, wondering at a past she was not part of. No one dared tell Thekla. This was all that remained of them.

"How many, Aunt Eva?"

"How many what?"

"Years. You said *many years ago.* How old are you?"

Eva had intended to lead Helena slowly toward the matter of the gifts. Now Helena had preempted her plan. She should not be surprised; she wondered that Helena hadn't asked long before for these personal details. None of them stood a chance where Helena was concerned. Eva steeled herself. As soon as she revealed her age, her niece would demand some answers. Eva had to be certain she was ready to give them.

"I am one hundred and two years old." Eva watched Helena's eyes flicker as she calculated the date.

"And Aunt Thekla?"

"One hundred and ten."

Helena took a step back and inspected her aunt's face. Eva didn't seem to be lying. Helena folded her arms in front of her chest and waited.

Eva knew that posture well. It was one that had sent at least two tutors through the front door, never to be seen again. Some could not cope with the gifted or the things they did when denied. Helena was waiting for information and would not move until she got it. Eva could hear her thoughts—*it isn't natural, it can't be true*—and wondered if Helena would even believe her.

"We are a rather unique family. A gifted family, in fact." Eva paused. "We are able to give unusual gifts, but only within our own family. Someone once gave us the gift of very long lives." As Eva suspected would happen, more questions rapidly followed.

"Will I grow so old, too?"

"Yes, you most likely will. We might live twice the number of years expected, but rarely more. It is not so bad." Eva lied. She thought it was awful, but Helena was young and had a whole life yet to live, gods willing. No need to spoil it now.

"Since we all live so long, where is your mother?" Helena had been told of her own mother's death, but appeared to feel little for the woman who had given birth to her.

"She died many years ago. It was her heart." Something you know nothing about, Eva wanted to add, but did not.

"We can die at any time, just like anyone else?"

"Yes, that's right. We are not immortal. We only have a longer lifespan than is usual. Such gifts are not given any longer. We give gifts to one person, rather than to the entire family. The gifts we give to that person must die with them. We cannot, sadly, do much about the gifts that have been given to us. We cannot take back the long life that your own child, for instance, will have. Eva was uncomfortable speaking of death and dying, but these were things Helena had to know.

"How many gifts can we get?"

Eva was not surprised to find that Helena had thoughts only for what she might get, rather than what she could give.

The full import of Eva's words was not sinking in. Eva chose to ignore it. Helena would know what the power to give meant when it finally came to her. After all, she was family too.

"As many as there are members of the family to give them, though we do try to establish limits."

Eva found she enjoyed sharing their legacy with Helena. It was a good one; they had nothing to be ashamed of. Thekla refused to speak of it. The more Helena knew, she said, the more likely it would be she'd discover the truth on her own, and none of them wanted that. In her excitement, Eva left caution behind.

"You were fortunate, you got one from each of us—eight all told. You received music and dance, song and grace, wit and that beautiful face of yours."

Helena looked at her strangely. "Eight."

"Pardon me?" Eva was confused.

"There are seven of you. You said *eight*." She frowned at Eva's blank look. "Who gave me the eighth gift?"

"Oh." Oh dear. It was too late to turn back now. Eva drew in her breath and straightened her shoulders. "We have another sister."

Saying the words felt like giving birth. Not as painful, surely, but at least as dangerous as the act itself and as relieving as the moment it was over. "An older sister."

"Older than Aunt Thekla? Where is she?"

"I don't know," Eva lied.

"What's wrong with her gift?"

"Wrong with it?"

"It doesn't work, like song or dance."

"Ah." Eva squirmed. "Well."

She wanted to take the easy way out, say Kitty simply hadn't given it to her yet, but that was the coward's path. This was her only chance to be brave without Thekla standing behind her and besides, Helena would see straight through that lie.

"She gave you the gift when you were a baby and then hid it from us all."

"Hid it? What do you mean, hid it?"

"I mean it is hidden. We don't know how it will manifest, or when or where."

"How do I find it?"

Eva wished she had an answer. "It is Kitty's gift. Only she can tell you that."

Neither of them moved as things in corners shifted, birds fluttered in the rafters and the ever-present dust drifted purposefully from one box to another. They stared at each other in the attic's dim light. Eva thought, *She is cold*. Helena thought, *She is old*.

Eva observed; she was good at it. Her motto had always been *I see and keep silent*. Since Helena's birth she had learned to act on her observations, and now Eva could no longer even claim silence as her own. I've done it, she thought, as she saw hunger dilate Helena's eyes. She will not rest now until she has opened Kitty's gift.

CHAPTER 15

HELENA STOOD IN A CIRCLE OF LIGHT AS AUNT EVA'S STEPS faded away. The attic loomed around her, awash with possessions stored or forgotten throughout countless years. It held the family's history, so Eva had said, and Helena was suddenly very interested in the lives of her aunts. She was a god who had just seen the face of her makers. She wasn't entirely pleased.

They had known all along how she was made and could have simply told her. Instead, they had let her starve. She was always so *hungry*. She had her own rituals, things she'd devised to sate her gifts, though beauty was hard to please once the mirrors had come down. She stretched herself as best as she was able in whatever direction her gifts chose.

Death was now mostly satisfied with knowledge; she could talk for hours about rites of burial in whatever culture she pleased without having to enact them. When she sat at the piano the house stopped to listen, and her voice lured the birds from the trees. She existed in unsteady harmony with seven of her gifts, but the eighth remained unsatisfied.

The gift Helena called life growled with displeasure. It begged to be used and bowed Helena under its weight. Even in her dreams she was constantly searching for whatever it was life needed. And now here came Eva, blithely admitting that they had known all along how Helena had been made. They knew she could not feed the gift because she did not yet possess it. *They knew*. She said it like a mantra, over and over, until repetition soothed the beast.

The attic was dark. Helena pulled another cord and a far light came on, slowly as though weakened with age. Its yellow aura seeped out into the cluttered space. The room ran the length of the south wing and was cool and dry. Helena sneezed and ducked as a bird whirred over her head.

The dust was thick and the air was dry and every time she moved she knocked into something else. A dressmaker's doll staggered away from her shoulder; she caught it before it fell. She bumped her toe on a chair, so covered in boxes and bolts of fabric that she hadn't seen it there. Most of the things were impersonal; she didn't care whose shoe that was, lying on its side, or who wore the silly hat festooned with ribbons now decaying on its brim. The further in she went, the more it seemed this was just a bunch of junk discarded by the family. It should all have been thrown away. Maybe she would tell Thekla it was here, just to see her reaction.

Nothing spoke to her of the sisters, neither the aunts she had been with since birth, nor the one she'd never known existed. It seemed odd that the seven of them remained close while the eighth was hidden. *Like her gift*, Helena thought. They obviously didn't want her to have it. They didn't want her to be a god. This was Thekla's doing and she knew it. Thekla was afraid of her gift.

Helena sought answers, but so far all she'd discovered

was a sure way to bruise her legs. Beauty did not like it, but Elfrieda would buy her a new necklace and that would make up for the marks.

Her aunts played a dangerous game. They might have made me, she thought, but they do not know what I am. Now she knew why she could not create life, and the blame lay squarely on them. It did not matter if they were frightened of her gift, they should have let her have it.

She was halfway across the long room, sandwiched between an overstuffed armchair and a muslin-draped piano, when she saw what she thought was a door. She made her way past more boxes, old instruments, toys, and open trunks until she reached the wall. It was not a door, but a painting with a frame so large it might be mistaken for one in the dull light of the attic. The canvas was faded and slightly warping and covered in a layer of grime. She wiped it away with her sleeve and touched the wood frame with her finger. It was cold. She looked into the faces peering out from the distant past.

A family was arranged in the downstairs ballroom, though the room was more lavishly appointed than her aunts would allow. Six small girls of varying ages were huddled beside the knees of a man in a grand, high-backed chair. He held a baby in his arms and was gazing at the others with a warm smile on his face. His wife—she must be—stood behind him with her hands placed upon his shoulders. To one side of her was a young woman, to the other, a young man. The pair seemed to belong together. Helena felt like an intruder just by looking at them.

They seemed such a happy family, huddled together with

smiles on their faces and kindly lights in their eyes. It could be an artist's trick, she thought, but somehow the very air around them seemed to vibrate with love. It was nothing like what Helena knew.

Helena counted: eight girls and one boy. Her face flushed; suddenly she recognized Thekla, already looking pained. She inspected the others more carefully and saw in them the rest of her aunts. Only the oldest of the eight girls was a stranger. Her eyes were the palest blue and looked out beyond Helena to the far side of the room, as though she was unaware of the artist's presence. She must be their older sister. Helena memorized her face and then let her eyes wander to the young man who must be their brother, someone else she knew nothing about.

Helena knelt in the dust of the attic and stared. His eyes were black as night, as was his hair, and his lips were a dull scarlet. She traced the shape of his face with her finger, could almost feel the velvet cloth around his neck. Something inside her lurched and reached out for him. The strain was immense. She flung herself away from the canvas as her stomach began to roil. Helena knelt in front of the painting as her hunger rose up inside her. She vomited and tears streamed from her eyes.

The painting waited while Helena shivered and curled into a ball. She lay in the dust and writhed like a snake fighting capture. She was seared by a need that had everything to do with her gifts. She had to have him. He was what life craved.

The painting was too large to carry, but she could no more leave his image in the attic than she could not breathe. The fit passed, she was able to rise to her feet, but slowly, as though her limbs were unsure of their function. She glanced around at the jumble of boxes. Surely there was something sharp up here somewhere. She would cut him out of the painting and leave the rest to rot.

She kicked a few piles of books aside and uncovered a rusty trowel. It would do. She gouged a hole in the canvas and sliced jaggedly around his shape. The trowel was old and its handle was loose. It slipped and sliced into her finger.

Helena snatched her hand away from the canvas and put her finger into her mouth as she had done when she was a child. She felt like a little girl just then, very small and helpless, but the moment passed and she pulled her finger out from between her lips. Another hack at the canvas with the trowel and it was done. She removed the piece and rolled it up gently, a treasure to be cherished. She turned out the lights behind her and made her way downstairs.

In her room, Helena unrolled the scrap of canvas. His eyes were on hers; she felt pulled in again. She retched with hunger, folded the canvas and tucked it away in a drawer. She wanted him as much as she wanted her gift, and didn't know where to find either.

CHAPTER 16

THAT NIGHT THEY GATHERED, SEVEN AGING SISTERS, MUCH as they'd done on the night of Helena's christening. It was a different place, a different time, but the matter at hand had not changed. Hope served the women coffee as Thekla began.

"I'm sure you all know by now why we're having this meeting." Thekla sent a pointed look in Eva's direction. "I am of a mind to seal the windows in the house. Some of you feel the need to discuss this first."

Thekla glared at Ingeburg as the others waited for her to finish. "I mean to have them boarded up immediately."

She steeled herself for their response.

Hilda and Helga leaned forward, their lack of astonishment proof that Eva had made the rounds. "It is not the windows, but the glass—just say it. We are not children, we know your motives."

"I cannot agree to this, Thekla. We do not even know what Kitty's gift will do." Zilli appeared prepared to jump straight into the fray.

"I seem to be the only one who still takes Kitty's curse seriously." Thekla aimed her ire at the twins. "And let me point out, it was you two who first thought it was glass we should fear."

"If you take it so seriously," Ingeburg countered, "why bring us here in the first place? Eva was right, you put us directly in Kitty's path."

"We *all* agreed to this plan. We have to be close to Kitty. Some of us don't share her particular vision." Thekla spat out the words as her skin mottled with anger.

"Yes, and we've been here for years. She's done nothing." Eva said. "May I remind you, Thekla, it was a *gift*, not a curse. There are safeguards to keep us from using our gifts for harm."

Eva was bluffing and Thekla knew it; there was no mechanism to prevent them from using their gifts as they liked, only their own good sense and the experience gained by their ancestors. Apparently they had not learned their lessons.

When Thekla held her silence, Eva tried another argument. "I hardly think the windows are a cause for alarm. You've stripped the house of all else, at least let it have its dignity."

"I cannot protect the child if you won't let me do it," Thekla was livid, her neck was taut and she sounded as if she ground salt between her teeth.

"You have protected her, but we are in this together, are we not? Surely if we pull together we can continue to do so without having to resort to such a drastic change to the house. I suggest one of us be with her at all times. We've always made sure she is never alone outside of the house. We can do the same with her inside." Eva caught her breath and then continued before Thekla could stop her.

"We must keep in mind, my sisters, that Helena is young.

It is natural she should eventually outgrow us. One day we will have to let her go, but for now let us join forces around her. Are we agreed?"

Thekla's jaw tightened. Eva had taken the meeting by storm. She was willing to have it done despite Eva's argument, but she saw she would be very much alone in her victory. Her sisters were joined against her. Perhaps it was a bit much. Eva's idea wasn't a bad one and would probably do for a while, but Kitty would quickly find a way around it. Helena's birthday was imminent, her sixteenth already. She'd be bored with her old aunts soon, if she weren't already. Perhaps something could be arranged.

"Fine," she said to her sisters. "Eva, you win. I will leave the windows. One of us will remain with Helena at all times. We will work out the details tomorrow, after a good night's rest."

Her sisters agreed to this, at least. Thekla watched them file out of the room until she was left alone in the pale light of a lamp. Shadows gathered in the corners as the sound of her sisters' feet slowly faded down corridors and halls and into the house beyond. It was an old house, a grand house, and perhaps Eva was right to want to preserve it. She was right about Helena, too. One day they would have to let her go.

Helena had grown into a beautiful young woman, but that was to be expected. Thick, dark hair fell around gently sloping shoulders, and she bore herself as though she were a queen. For sixteen years they'd lived their lives around her, waiting and watching and fearing the worst, yet somehow, Helena was still alien to them.

Thekla contemplated a future in which Helena was out of

their reach. There was, perhaps, an even better plan. Helena would one day have to leave the household, yes, but Thekla could decide when and where she would go.

℅℆

Helena waited until Thekla was gone, then slipped out from behind the thick velvet curtains drawn over the shuttered windows. *She was right.* They didn't want her to find Kitty's gift. All but one of them, she reminded herself. Aunt Eva, at least, seemed to be on her side. Helena looked at the windows behind her and wondered what they had to do with any of this. Her aunts were hiding all manner of things from her and from each other. That was even more fascinating, though it brought her no closer to finding her gift or the means of using it.

She would have to speak with Aunt Eva again, though Eva would only tell her what she thought Helena should know. No tantrum would change that. She wondered how Kitty would respond to her questions, and had a sudden idea.

Her aunts played such a fine game with her life. It would be a terrible shame not to join them.

She was in the music room, Eva on guard nearby, when she made her move. "I'll be sixteen years old in a few days,"

"Are you sure? It seems just yesterday you were born."

Helena's supple hands glide over the keys; the piece was simple, alluring, original.

"You aren't senile yet. You know perfectly well how old I'll be." Helena was not in the mood for joking. The music took a turn; it deepened and suggested danger.

106

"You are right, of course," Eva said, rebuked,

"What does Aunt Thekla have planned?" Helena flashed her bright smile.

"It is going to be quite the event, I hear. She has invited over one hundred guests, if you can believe it. Every relative you can think of and then some, every tutor you've ever had. Thekla has demanded nothing but the best for you on your sweet sixteenth. She's taken care of every detail herself."

Thekla was probably trying to make up for her bad behavior, Helena thought. "Good. More presents for me."

Helena let the music trail off, as if that was all, and then, "Has she invited your sister?" The lighthearted tune continued. She didn't expect Eva to answer, and was surprised when she did.

Eva seemed to know exactly who Helena meant. "No."

"Why not?" Helena lifted her hands away from the keys and turned to face her aunt.

"We don't know where she is." Eva failed to buy herself just a little more time with this lie.

"Yes, you do. You all know exactly where she is. I heard you talking about her, and about me." Helena lifted her shoulders, dared Eva to contradict her.

"I want her to come to my party. If she doesn't, I will tell Thekla what you've told me and see what she has to say about my gift."

Shock slide across Eva's features. She eased stiff fingers over swollen knuckles and shifted her weight in the chair.

"You are right. We do know where Kitty is. I will ask her to come to your party. Who knows? Perhaps she will bring your

ERZEBET YELLOWBOY

gift with her."

Eva smoothed her skirt and rose. "The twins will sit with you next."

"Wait." Helena wasn't finished with her. "Tell me about your brother."

Eva sat back down in the chair and closed her eyes. "How do you know about our brother?"

"I have my ways," Helena smiled wickedly.

Eva seemed to too tired to argue. "What would you like to know?"

"What was his name? Why don't you talk about him?"

"Louis. His name was Louis. He died when he was eighteen years old. There is nothing to talk about."

Helena's gift opened hungry jaws and snapped at the air in front of her. She had assumed he was much like their oldest sister, a secret sibling they had chosen not to share. It never occurred to her he might be dead, like their mother. She was ruined. There was no hope. Life surged and pleaded for sustenance. She turned his name over on her tongue, remembered his eyes and could not accept his condition. The moment passed and Helena suddenly smiled. Once she had Kitty's gift, she could fix that.

"Thank you, Aunt Eva. That will be all."

Helena's stomach howled, her pores opened and hunger carved his name on her bones. I must have the gift, she thought, so I can have Louis. Without him I will die.

CHAPTER 17

THE SISTERS GATHERED IN THE WIDE BALLROOM, A HUGE room that spanned most of the north wing of the house. Ladders dotted the open space, some in use by a team of men who were threading stars of silver and gold onto a long wire. Two others hung a large crystal globe in the center of the room. The entire solar system was suspended from the ceiling, lit by the lamp of the sun.

Thekla was smiling and chatting with the men as though she were young again. The plans had been laid; she had a special present prepared for Helena this year. Her sisters could keep their precious windows and hang mirrors all over the walls if they liked, for it would no longer matter. Tomorrow Helena was leaving and none of them were the wiser. Nor would they be, until she announced it at Helena's party.

"Everything is so lovely. You have outdone yourself, Thekla." Eva startled her from her reverie.

"Thank you. It was hardly all my idea, however. I had plenty of help from my sisters." Thekla smiled pleasantly.

Eva snorted. "May we speak for a moment?"

"What is it? We can talk right here," Thekla spoke hurriedly. "I must see to the catering."

"It is about our sister." Eva nodded her head at Thekla's questioning look.

Thekla frowned and reached for her cane. "The library."

They left the room as amiably as two dear old friends, but when they reached the library, Thekla threw down her cane in disgust. "What is it?"

"Tomorrow is Helena's sixteenth birthday. It will be the grandest party we've ever held. I recall another event to which a certain person was not invited. I do not think we should make that mistake again." Eva paused. "Invite Kitty to Helena's party. Let us keep her as close as possible."

Thekla stared at Eva as though she was a stranger. She needed a moment to think. Helena's sixteenth . . . For no reason she could discern, Thekla suddenly put a date to the day. Why hadn't she thought of it before? If anything were to happen, it would certainly be tomorrow! Helena, Thekla suddenly recalled, shared her date of birth with Kitty. Thekla shuddered as she remembered something else. It had been at Kitty's own sixteenth birthday celebration that things had first gone wrong.

Thekla recalled the way in which Katza had run from the ballroom, following Louis. Thekla had watched them carry Katza in afterwards, soaked through with rain. Louis had never returned. As far as Thekla knew, none of them had seen him alive again after Katza's party.

Thekla cringed. She must have been blind not to see it. Katza and Louis, as close as any lovers, must have fought at the party one hundred years ago. He ran out. She followed, fell and hit her head on the flagstones. Louis drowned and they found his body the next day. Thekla tapped her fingers on the table while Eva waited in silence.

Kitty was linked to their brother's death. No wonder her sister was obsessed with changing the past. Thekla's rage boiled over. It was Kitty's black heart that had destroyed the family. There was only one way to stop her from doing it again.

"I will go. Make certain the front room is locked when the men are finished."

Thekla wasted no time. She trampled the garden path and crossed the courtyard, never heeding the wood or the placid flowers or how the clouds crossed the sky. The door to Kitty's house swung open before she reached it; she was not surprised. Thekla stopped on the step and smiled up at her sister.

"As you most likely know, we are celebrating Helena's sixteenth birthday tomorrow. As it is also your birthday, I'd like to invite you to join us."

Kitty puffed up, as though embracing the defiance evident in her sister. "I would be delighted, thank you."

"The party begins at six o'clock sharp." Thekla turned to leave. "Do try to be a bit early."

"Oh, don't worry." Kitty said as she shut the door. "I will be."

Thekla laughed on the step like a child. She had a present for both Helena and Kitty.

Neither of them would ever see it coming.

CHAPTER 18

KITTY LEANED HER HEAD AGAINST THE HARD WOOD OF THE door once Thekla passed out of sight. Everything was falling into place nicely—this time she would not fail.

She tasted the air; it was fresh and damp. She was blessed to have come from this land, she thought, this wonderful place of tall trees and castles in the sky. This time she would remember that.

She drew in her breath and climbed the stairs. She hadn't been to a party in ages. Whatever would she wear? At her age, did such things even matter? She did want to go out in style. Kitty replayed the past one more time, for the last time. It hurt, but she had to do it. Tomorrow it would be gone.

The words her brother had spoken one hundred years ago had stunned her.

"Katza, he has asked for me. I must go to him."

Katza had been furious. She had tolerated his little romance because she had no other option, but now—a meeting with the king was dangerous at any time, but on this, of all nights! It was insulting and it had wounded her deeply. Did Louis not understand? Had he been so blinded by Ludwig's glory that he would turn away from *her*, his beloved sister? She had gritted her teeth to the point of breaking. Once upon a time, Louis had loved her. Only her. Now he would leave her for an unlikely meeting with the king.

"It is my birthday, Louis. You cannot just run off into the night. You must stay here. Besides, how do you even know it was really the king who sent the message?"

"It has his seal."

Her hands had clenched so fiercely that her nails had pierced her flesh. She knew he wouldn't have mentioned it, had she not gone into his coat pocket and found the letter herself. He had grabbed it from her hand before she had finished reading it, but she had seen enough. Louis had been ever impractical, but since the king's visit he seemed to have lost his mind.

She had wondered if she should finally tell Papa of Louis' infatuation. Mama and Papa were romantics at heart, like their son, and Katza had doubted it would do any good. She had ended up watching the hours roll past with a feeling of sick helplessness. She had made and discarded plans to follow her brother and had paced through the house like a wild thing caught in a cage.

She had tried to talk him out of it one last time.

"Louis, you must not do this. You cannot know the letter came from him." She had been hysterical enough to grab his shirtfront. "Louis, you must come to my party!"

"I will be there for you," he had said with a sigh, "but I cannot stay. This may be the only chance I have to see him. I love him—why can't you accept that? Is it because he is a man? Katza, I can never be with him in truth. Let me have this one moment, please?"

Katza had faced defeat. There would be no reasoning with her brother.

She had hoped, even prayed, that Louis would put this mood behind him, but ever since he'd met the king he'd been obsessed with seeing him again. *No,* she had answered Louis silently. *It is not because he is a man. It is because you no longer love me.* She had seen then that Louis would follow this to its end, no matter what she said.

She had bowed her head. "Just remember, Louis, that I am the one who loves you." There was nothing else she could have done to stop him, not then.

Louis had made his appearance at her party, as promised. His face had been drawn and he'd hovered in the corner against a backdrop of sweeping, blue curtains. Beautiful and tense, his shoulders had been hunched against the guests who swirled around him. They had seemed to know better than to attempt any conversation.

There had been entertainment and food and brightly dressed ladies pulling disgruntled men through the halls, children laughing and girls dancing and Katza had seen no one but Louis. He had watched her watch him, offered a wan smile, raised a glass, but Katza had been unmoved. She had glared at him, so much so that her mother had asked her if something was wrong.

"No, Mama. Everything is fine, it is a lovely party," she had smiled sweetly.

Magdalena had gone off to greet a guest and Katza had been left with her anger.

She'd waited for Louis to leave. Five o'clock, six

o'clock . . . she had glanced behind her and been caught for a moment by her reflection in a mirror on the far wall. When she'd turned around he'd been gone. She had run past a group of girls, by a maid with a tray of fruit, through the kitchens where the cook had been shouting and out the door to the gardens. Rain had been pouring from the dark sky, clouds had clotted overhead and her lungs had filled with moisture as she called out her brother's name.

She had heard a horse and the sound of Louis' voice commanding the beast to run.

She had chased after him; the ground had been wet and she'd slipped on the flagstones just in front of the stable. She had turned wildly and her hair, loosened from its usual braid for the celebration, had whipped across her eyes. She'd fallen and hit her head on the stones.

Katza's family had found her in the courtyard, still crumpled on the stones. She'd woken hours later, in the middle of the night, in pain but mostly unharmed. Louis had been at her side.

"Is it you, Louis?" Katza had been disoriented until her brother's features had settled into place.

"I am here, Katza. All is well." He had smoothed the hair back from her brow. "I will tell Mama you are awake. Rest now."

She never saw Louis again.

The next day, when the family had gathered for breakfast, Louis was absent. Katza had felt fine; no evidence remained of her fall. The familiar sound of Papa rattling the newspaper had drawn her to the table. As she had reached her seat, an attendant had rushed in and handed Papa a letter.

"My God," Papa had suddenly shouted into the quiet morning.

Mama, Katza and Thekla had turned towards him as the other children had giggled on in their corner, unconcerned by the look on Papa's face.

"What is it?" Mama had asked, her hand on his arm.

"The king," Papa had cried. "Ludwig was found in the lake last night. They say it might have been murder!"

No one had seen Louis enter the room and no one had seen him leave it, though he must have been there to hear Papa's exclamation.

Later that day, in Louis' room, Katza had rediscovered the king's letter. By then they'd realized Louis was missing and the staff, with Papa, had been out in the forests searching for him. The letter must have fallen from Louis' pocket in the night. She had read every word with horror.

Hide yourself well—I have many enemies. Two of them will be there, plotting against me. Kill them for me, Louis, and I will meet you after.

The king had been very precise in his description of the surrounding terrain. He had made it easy for Louis to find the perfect place to do the deed. The trees had been thick by the water, the castle had loomed in the distance and two men must have walked the path, just as the king had described.

She had seen it then: Louis takes aim, his rifle at the ready. Clouds gather and cover the moon, but Louis can still see his targets in front of him. He waits until they enter the water, just as the king has instructed, where they are watching for a boat.

Louis is an excellent shot. He fires twice and, when Ludwig doesn't appear, he goes home.

Katza had put her head in her hands and cried. The king had tricked Louis. That evening she had learned that Louis had returned to the lake and shot himself by the shore. This was the past that Katza had not prevented.

This was the past she was finally going to change.

CHAPTER 19

THE DAY OF HELENA'S PARTY DAWNED CLEAR AND BRIGHT, though grey clouds hovered over the Alps in the distance. The lake was dark and a breeze shook the upper limbs of the trees that clustered around it. Kitty enjoyed a breakfast of sausage and eggs and then read a book to help pass the time. In mid-afternoon she washed with care, drew a fresh slip over her head and chose her finest stockings and garter. She combed out her hair, still thick and full, and slowly began to braid it.

It was a fine gift Kitty had been given, to be able to bend time backward or forward. She could make of it an acrobat touching the back of her hands to her ankles, one moment pressing upon one another until they merged, and back became front and front became back, twisting inside out and upright again.

When she was young her gift had seemed no more than a parlor trick, a way to tease Papa by moving his papers or books back to where they'd been a week before. This, her family tolerated.

When she had moved a stable hand two hours ahead, it was a different matter. The man had been trampled beneath a startled horse and had never walked again. As if that hadn't been bad enough, Louis' displeasure had almost killed her. She never wanted to see that look on his face again.

Kitty's gift did have one safeguard. Her attempts to move herself in time all failed. If she was lucky, nothing at all would happen, but sometimes she ended with a headache that sent her to bed for three days. Her Sight was one thing, a bonus received in a fall. Her gift was another. If only she could get to the places she *Saw*.

For all the years after Papa died, she had pondered time and ways around the limits of her gift. She had a simple plan. She would return to the past and somehow save her brother. Katza had to accept, at last, that this was impossible. Her body simply could not be transported. Someone would have to return in her place and that had been absolutely unthinkable.

The question had then become one of *when*. Forget for a moment, she told herself, about physicality. If she could go back, what moment offered the best chance of success? When Louis had first told her he was in love, she had nothing to say that might change his mind. He would never believe she'd returned from the future to warn him away from the king. The night of the king's visit the spell had been cast, but she could not again face the sight of Louis and Ludwig together. That had left the night of Katza's sixteenth birthday party, before Louis had departed, and suddenly she'd had an answer.

Katza recalled the night she had seen the old hag, herself speaking to herself by way of a looking glass. And at her party, for just a moment, she'd been caught by her reflection again. It was exactly the moment she needed, but appearing in a mirror was simply not good enough. It left far too much to chance. She must, somehow, pass *through* the mirror. She must connect with herself—become herself—for only she, old and grey, knew what would happen after.

Finally, a possibility had come to her. Her body might be fixed, but the mind was another matter. She supposed her gift would not allow for that sort of travel either, and even if it did work, Kitty knew her mind could only be in one place at one time. She could not exist both now and then, but Kitty had refused to be daunted. No matter the cost, she could not let her brother commit murder. She had to find a way to trick her gift, to make it seem as though she meant it for someone else. Who would best serve her purpose? She had fretted and stewed for many long years, until finally the poppet had revealed herself.

Kitty smiled as she buttoned her favorite dress. When dealing with time, one must be precise. Helena, born one hundred years to the hour after Kitty's own birth, was precisely what Kitty needed. Helena was the perfect mirror; she would reflect Kitty's gift back onto Kitty and come to no harm herself. Helena only had to look into the glass; the gift would do the rest.

Kitty watched the future speed toward her. Had she not prophesied it herself those sixteen years ago? After all of this time, it was now only a matter of hours.

CHAPTER 20

HELENA WOKE LATE IN THE MORNING TO THE SOUND OF birdsong coming from the open window. She leaned over the edge of her bed, picked up a shoe and threw it at the sparrow on the sill. Startled, it flew off. She stretched luxuriously, greedily, and gathered the linens under her chin and rolled in them.

Another birthday, the day her distant devotees gathered to make their offerings. Their pilgrimage ended on her doorstep and resulted in a great many presents. Helena enjoyed the annual ritual, but this year the usual assortment of clothing and books, jewelry and junk hardly mattered. All she could think of was Kitty's gift and that she would finally have it. She wrapped a robe around her shoulders. Her appetite was huge.

The kitchen doors were locked. She pounded on one and waited for Hope, ever so slow, to open it. She strode past the old maid, who let the door close behind her as Helena sat at the table. Hunks of meat and cheeses were spread out on cutting boards and vegetables were stacked beside bowls of flour and spices. The knife Hope was using to cut the meat lay carelessly on its side. Helena raised it to her face, held it in front of her like a mirror and gazed into its blade. She frowned and threw it back down. She could find no beauty in that.

"I want something to eat."

"Happy birthday," Hope said as she reached for a fresh loaf of bread.

Helena gulped down a glass of milk. "What are you going to give me? Not the same old knitted sweater, I hope."

"The very same."

"What color this year?"

"Red. It is a good color, don't you think?"

"I'm getting a better gift than that. You can keep the sweater, I don't want it." Helena smiled, her teeth perfectly white and even behind wide, scarlet lips.

Hope buttered the bread.

"Don't you want to know what it is?" Helena teased.

"Not particularly." Hope slid a plate of bread slathered with cherry jam towards Helena, who devoured it within minutes while watching Hope slice an apple.

Hope never changed. She cut things up and put them together, day after day, and every year gave Helena the most useless gifts. Hope's nature disturbed Helena. She was too simple to comprehend.

"What do you know about the gifts my aunts gave me?"

The question did not surprise Hope; she'd expected it years ago. She wasn't going to give Helena the answers she sought, but Hope did say enough to distract her.

"It was during your christening. People arrived from all over the world—it's a wonder the house held so many. It wasn't as large as this one. You were a little darling. Everyone loved you immediately."

Helena looked at Hope strangely. Her aunts had never spoken of her so. "We didn't live in this house?"

"No dear, we lived in America."

"I wasn't born here?" Helena's opinion of Hope was instantly revised. She knew things and was willing to share them. "I was born in another country?"

"That's right." Hope wiped the table.

"You were at my christening." Helena watched Hope's face. "You probably knew about the gifts, too."

Hope was relieved when Thekla entered the kitchen, her face flush with excitement and her breath coming short. She interrupted the pair without notice.

"There you are. I want to talk to you about your party." Thekla swept towards Helena, her head held high.

Helena wrinkled her nose. Thekla acted as though she loved Helena's parties as much as Helena did.

Thekla gathered her skirts and sat carefully on a chair. She looked like she'd been awake for hours already, fretting and worrying about the evening to come. Her hair was slightly disheveled and her breath came in quick gasps.

She cleared her throat. "Listen carefully. The guests will begin to arrive at four o'clock and you must be available to greet them. The party starts promptly at six. I will be making an important announcement and it is crucial you hear it."

"What kind of announcement?"

Helena had expected the usual boring toasts and speeches. This must be something special.

"I can tell you no more," Thekla smiled innocently, "but it has to do with one of your presents."

Helena felt a surge of hunger and reached for another plate of food. Could it be true? Would Thekla change her mind and reveal the gift? Excitement charged through her. All of them were scheming and for the first time in her life, Helena felt as though she might not be the spider, but something caught in its web. It made her a little sick, but she squashed it. All that mattered was that she find Kitty's gift and she would, this very night. Helena's priorities fell like beads on an abacus and settled into place.

"I'll be in my room, should anyone want me. I will not have a chaperone today." Helena let the door slam shut behind her.

The guests began to arrive in late afternoon as predicted. The sunny morning had turned dark and grey by noon; rain now lashed from heavy skies, but that did not stop them. Helena watched from her bedroom window as Herr Krieger, stalwart old historian, climbed the stairs to the front door. He wore the same frown on his face as he did to her lessons. Most of the guests would be family, but her tutors would be there and they always knew what she liked. She'd get good gifts, but none would compare to Kitty's.

She opened the wardrobe and clothes spilled out around her. She reached for the dress she'd ordered: lush velvet of the darkest crimson, a strap over one shoulder, skin-tight. Her aunts didn't like it, but they could not say no. Helena brushed out her hair one last time, smoothed the dress over her hips and went lightly down the great, curving stair to the hallway where her aunts greeted the guests. She was caught and held as they streamed past in a happy blur of kisses, handshakes and stale perfume. She waved each one by, paying scarce attention to any, when suddenly a hush fell over the crowd. Helena turned towards the door and froze in place.

The woman entering was old as gravedust, but her eyes glittered with life as they focused on Helena's face. Something in Helena was jarred out of place; she felt the ground give way beneath her feet. Aunt Kitty waited for a kiss.

Thekla broke the silence. "Kitty, please join us."

Only Eva had known Kitty was invited; the other sisters gasped and stuttered as they nodded their greetings. Kitty passed by quickly and stopped in front of Helena.

"My goodness," she said, "how you've grown."

Seven sisters drew in their breaths.

"You've seen me before." Helena recovered her balance. She was looking forward to this.

"I was at your christening, dear girl. I apologize for staying away so very long." She smiled graciously at Thekla and bowed her head. Her sisters sighed as one.

"I am very pleased to meet you," Helena's impeccable manners were a lure for the unwary, but Kitty did not play children's games.

Kitty spoke quietly into Helena's ear. "You and I must talk."

Before Helena could stop her, Kitty walked away.

The stream of guests finally came to an end and Helena entered the ballroom, dazzled by what she saw. Above her head, planets turned while stars spun their light into high corners. Black cloth covered the ceiling; the only thing visible in the heights was the cosmos, gaily turning above the milling guests.

The mountain of presents was enormous, but tempting as they appeared, she knew none were what she wanted.

She scanned the crowd for her oldest aunt, but didn't see her anywhere. The buffet table was laden with enough food to fill everyone's bellies two or three times. Guests plucked at delicacies, piled hunks of meat upon their plates and drank of hearty fresh beer and the fine aged wines dredged up from the well-secured cellars. Thekla sat in a cushioned chair behind the high table on which the presents were piled. She was a queen surveying her court, and what a grand court it was. Helena even saw Hope, standing next to Aunt Ingeburg. She looked like a tarnished clasp in a necklace of diamonds. *Poor Hope*, Helena laughed. She tried, but she didn't belong there.

CHAPTER 21

HOPE RARELY LEFT HER KITCHEN, IT WAS TRUE, BUT SHE
had her reasons. The kitchen was Hope's storehouse and she
didn't feel comfortable out of it. She did what she had to in
the other rooms of the house—dusted lightly, changed linens,
swept out the halls and served coffee—but she was content to
spend most of her time at the great kitchen table. It was there
that she'd lined up her ingredients and filled the little leather
pouch. It was there that she'd spoken ancient words over it. It
was there that Thekla had leaned toward her and said, "Don't
let Helena out of your sight."

Hope studied the ballroom carefully, took note of the guests
and watched Helena as she peered through the room, obviously
searching for someone. Hope knew what was happening.
Kitty was there to unleash her monster, but Kitty was in for a
surprise. Hope was skilled at hiding herself, especially from
eyes such as Kitty's. Hope squinted in Helena's direction and
reached for the pouch at her neck.

Dread filled her—it wasn't there. She had worked years of
magic in preparation for this night and then forgotten the
pouch in the kitchen. Age gets us all in the end, she thought,
before going to retrieve it.

Helena watched Hope leave the ballroom. She was just about to turn and follow when she heard someone whisper her name.

"Helena."

Helena caught it between two conversations and followed it to its source. It was Aunt Eva.

"Come with me. Kitty would like a word with you." Eva held out her hand. Her face was expressionless.

"I thought she was waiting for Thekla's announcement." A thrill went through Helena's body; she rubbed her hands together without realizing it.

"Announcement? What are you talking about? Kitty would like to speak with you privately, if you do not mind."

Helena eagerly followed Aunt Eva. Thekla probably hadn't told them that she had changed her mind about Kitty's gift. It was just more of her aunts' deviousness, Helena thought angrily. Instead of joining hands around their god in devotion, as any sensible followers should, they fought over which one followed best.

The crowd paid them no attention as it parted and reformed around them. No one noticed their exit, not even Thekla, who was trying to keep her eye on everyone all at once. At the back of the house they entered an empty room. Rarely used, it contained little more than a long sofa and a few cushioned chairs. Wide, tall windows looked out onto the dead roses. Their feeble stems scratched against the glass as a quick wind blew by the house. On one of the chairs sat Kitty, legs crossed, hands folded in her lap. Eva, red-faced, shut the door behind her as she left them alone in the room.

"My dear Helena. I am so glad to see you again." She smiled, a red slash carved into a wrinkled face that might have scared a different girl.

"Why?" Helena was intrigued.

"Because I am your aunt, that is why."

"Where is my gift?" Helena wondered if Kitty would make it as difficult as the rest of them did.

Kitty surprised Helena. She reached behind her neck and undid the clasp of a chain that she pulled from beneath the collar of her dress. She lifted it free of the folds and Helena saw, dangling from its end, a small silver key. Kitty held it out.

Helena took it in her hand, studied its shape. "What does it open?"

"It unlocks a door, Helena."

"What will I find when I open it?" Helena already knew, but she wanted to hear Kitty say it.

"The gift you seek, of course. It is time for you to have it."

Helena's hand closed over the key. She would not let Kitty know that every bone in her body was screaming for her to use it. There was one more thing to ask before she did.

"Tell me about your brother."

Kitty's smile fell just a little and she hesitated before she spoke. Helena watched the rise and fall of her chest intently, wondering at the vast age with which her aunt confronted her.

Kitty sighed. "He was very kind, and very young when he died. That is the past, Helena. Attend to the present."

"Where do I find the door?" Helena held up the key. She was too impatient for more. She was shaking with hunger for it, and for him.

"It is through another, just there behind you." Kitty looked down at her wristwatch.

"You have just enough time to open it."

Helena turned her head to look behind her. All she saw was the window. She looked back at Kitty, who nodded.

"It is there."

Helena put her hands on the glass and looked up at the curtain rod stretched above the frame. The curtains moved, though the windows were closed. She went over to them, brushed them aside and revealed a slender door. She rattled the ancient handle. The door opened onto a stairway leading into the wall.

"Should I go up?" she turned to ask Kitty, as though unsure.

"Yes."

※ ※

In the ballroom, Thekla surveyed the crowd with pleasure. Her announcement was sure to shock Helena, but she'd soon come around. Thekla had pulled every string she knew how to pull, made offers and moved mountains. Helena was going away; the university was pleased to have her and they understood her special needs. Thekla stroked the table in front of her, ran one gnarled finger along its edge. It held Helena's presents and more. Thekla laughed. She would foil Kitty's curse altogether and still send Helena off to school, and there was nothing Kitty could possibly do to stop her.

Louis had taken the best care of his rifle; Thekla had watched him clean it so many times she had memorized the procedure. Thekla had never liked the device. It was ugly and loud, but it was also a part of Louis. It had been found on the lakeshore, near his body. No one knew Thekla had kept it.

Upon their return to Bayern, she had taken it from its hiding place, cleaned it, oiled it, and made sure it was in good working order. She hadn't even been sure why she'd done it until now. She had practiced her aim in her room late last night, got used to the rifle's awkward weight. The rifle was loaded and today she was ready to use it.

Thekla looked through the room for her grandniece—it was almost six o'clock. The blood rushed from her face as her eyes flitted from person to person.

Neither Helena nor Kitty was there.

No.

Thekla reached under the table.

She was so close.

She could not let Kitty win now.

Thekla wished for the strength of youth as she clutched the rifle and hurried painfully down the hall. She heard a voice and followed it.

Kitty sat with her legs crossed, calmly smiling. She did not seem surprised to see Thekla.

Thekla raised the rifle and aimed it at Kitty's head. She curled her finger around the trigger. "Where is Helena?"

ജ

Two old women gazed at each other across the span of years. They were old, they were young, they were old again.

Kitty looked into Thekla's eyes and thought of all of the years lost between them, and then let them go. She was prepared to die.

It was the only way Louis could live.

WHAT A STRANGE PLACE TO PUT A GIFT, THOUGH AT LEAST here it was well hidden from Thekla. And from herself, Helena thought as she felt her way up the stairs. Certain that life was a part of her, like beauty and grace and the others, she puzzled over the nature of a gift kept behind a locked door. She reached the top without finding an answer. There was a ledge along the wall. Her hands passed over a book of matches and beside them, a candle in a round holder. She put a flame to the wick and it lit with a flare, revealing another small door. She rattled the handle—this one was locked. She looked at the key in her hand.

It fit snugly into the lock and turned with ease. The small room was cold and bare, except for a mirror that hung across from her, and a tiny window high up in the wall. Helena put her nose as close as she could to the mirror without doubling her vision and clutched either side of the frame. She saw herself clearly for the first time in years.

A gift opened ravenous jaws.

Hunger surged and sent a shock through her body. She felt faint and clung to the frame. The nail Karl had hammered in to hold the mirror was unable to bear her weight and gave way. She and the mirror both fell to the floor. The mirror broke into a hundred pieces. Helena lay among them as though dead.

ℬℭ

Downstairs, four women heard the glass shatter.

Kitty's eyes widened. Her spell wouldn't work with the mirror broken and she had never foreseen this.

Thekla was startled. Her finger involuntarily tightened on the trigger and began to pull it back.

Eva had seen Thekla reach under the table, pull out a long object and hurry to the door to the hall. She had covered her mouth, wide in shock, when she'd seen what Thekla was holding.

Oh god, Eva had thought. She *is* mad.

Eva had rushed after her. When she entered the room to find her fears realized, she spoke without hesitation.

"I give the gift of sleep."

Like Kitty, she had never specified a recipient. Eva had no time to think; she opened her gift for them all.

Motes of dust halted in mid-flight, trapped as though weightless in the air. Outside, the roses shuddered. Inside, all slept in place. The rifle still aimed at Kitty's head. Kitty sat, eyes open, on the chair. In the grand ballroom the dancers turned and stopped, like suddenly wound-down toys.

Upstairs, Helena vanished.

ℬℭ

In the kitchen, Hope found her forgotten bundle and tied it around her neck. As she made the final knot in the cord she, too, heard the mirror break.

Hope expected the worst and was not surprised when she found it.

Upon entering that lonely room, a lesser woman might have fainted. Hope never dreamed Thekla owned a rifle, much less knew how to use one. Thank goodness she'd not been able to do so—Eva's counter-spell had suspended them all. Hope put her hand on Thekla's arm to remove the rifle.

It wouldn't budge; Thekla was hard as stone.

Hope touched the pouch at her neck in gratitude. She had devised several spells of her own to protect her from Helena's gifts. Helena's charm and grace never swayed Hope, her beauty went all but unseen, and when Eva's spell put the household to sleep, Hope had been unaffected. Though Hope had erred in leaving Helena, the success of her spell buoyed her up. It was good to find she had not lost her touch. There was still Kitty's gift to consider, but for that Hope relied on another.

No one, not even Kitty, could match wits with Hope's young charge. All Hope had to do was find her.

Hope quickly discovered the secret stair and chided herself for not knowing about it. She felt her way along the wall until she reached the top, where she stopped and caught her breath at the small door. It was unlocked. She pushed it open. Faint light from a sliver of window illuminated the room well enough for Hope to see the scattered fragments of mirror on the floor.

She bent down carefully, picked up a large piece of glass and held it to the light.

Hope rarely accepted a fact as a fact unless it came with strong evidence, but mirrors most often present their own proof. For vanity's sake they reflect an image. For magic's, they retain it. Hope turned the shard over in her hand.

This was certainly magic, and of the very worst kind.

What was Kitty doing? Ah well, Hope thought. She could not ask her now. Hope could see Helena's face in the thin broken glass, as though it had been painted there, but Kitty's spell did not end with mere reflection. Helena should have been standing in front of the mirror, frozen like everyone else. She could not have left the room—Hope would have seen her. Helena was nowhere. That meant there was only one place she could be.

Hope would not begin to guess at Kitty's motives, nor did they really matter at this point in time. Helena would figure it out, if only she could be reached. Whether Kitty intended for it or not, Helena had slipped through the mirror. She could only return from wherever she was if the glass could be repaired.

Back in the kitchen Hope gathered her tools: a lamp, a glue pot, a paintbrush, a stool for her to sit on, newspaper on which she could do her work. She returned to the secret room, basket of goods in hand, and made herself as comfortable as possible. Hope sang to herself as she pieced the mirror together, used the brush to line jagged edges with glue and laid them out on the paper. The mirror spread beneath her hands as the past rushed up behind her. She saw Helena in every shard she touched.

CHAPTER 23

THEKLA WAS OUT OF BED EARLY ON THE MORNING OF KATZA'S sixteenth birthday, haunting the kitchen in search of a fresh bun or two. Louis was there before her with his gun, a long, gleaming rifle that made Thekla nervous. She knew he was proud of his skills, but the thing made an awful noise when fired that always hurt her ears.

"Where are you hunting today?" she asked in the hope he would stay for a moment and talk with her.

Louis put his hand under her chin. "The same place as always, little sister, beside the lake. Why aren't you in bed? The sun has yet to shine and here you are, wide awake."

He smiled at her; it seemed to Thekla the sun didn't need to shine when Louis was in the room.

She rubbed her eyes. "I couldn't sleep. I had a dream."

"Was it a terrible dream?" The look in his eyes was kind, as though he knew how bad dreams could spill into one's waking.

"Very. There was a dragon sleeping in a forest and it was going to eat me when it woke up. I ran and ran but couldn't get away from it."

Louis looked into her eyes and gave her courage. "Dragons

do not eat little girls, I promise you that. In any case, the dream is done and you are with me, safe and sound. There are no dragons here."

"Will you stay and tell me a story?"

Louis shook his head. "I cannot. The sun will rise and chase all of the game away. When I return, you'll get your story. Will you wait?"

Thekla nodded, but Louis was already gone.

℘ ☙

Louis felt sorry for Thekla, but he was in a rush. He caressed the envelope concealed in his coat pocket. It had arrived the night before, delivered by a silent messenger on behalf of the king. Louis had recognized the seal as soon as his hand closed on the letter. His heart fluttered even now as he thought about it.

The bearer of the message did not know its contents; this was their little secret. Louis thought it proof he'd not been wrong about their feelings for each other, something he'd worried over ever since the night he and Ludwig met. He remembered it well.

The snow had blown in and covered his legs when he opened the kitchen door, but Louis never thought to brush it off. The man had been much larger than Louis imagined; his presence had flooded the room. The Magic King had been there, in the very ordinary kitchen, and he was an incredible figure. Louis did not see a man past his prime, or a man lost in the throes of madness. The king had seemed as sane as any other as he stood with his cloak dripping water onto the floor.

138

For the king it had been shelter from the storm, a haven in the dark night and adventure. For Louis, the king had personified love. After years of longing for the idea of the king, there he finally was, right in front of Louis. He would never recover from his first meeting with King Ludwig II. Impressionable and impressed, Louis had taken the sodden cloak from the attendant's hands and hung it on a hook by the fire. He could do nothing then but gaze upon his king.

It had all happened in a fog, like those that rolled over the lake in early morning. Louis hunted there, he knew how the air congealed on top of the water and followed the waves to shore. Ludwig had been attentive, the attendant silent, and an entire affair of the eyes had developed there in the steaming kitchen, beneath the iron pots that hung from the ceiling and the row of pastries set out to cool for the morning.

When Katza had appeared, like a random ghost, peeking through the door as though she were a child spying on her elders, Louis' had wanted to hide. He knew how much she'd seen—no secrets were kept from Katza—but when the door had shut lightly as she turned away, Louis forgot, until much later, that she had ever been there.

He was confident now that his feelings were reciprocated. The message was his proof. Louis hoisted his rifle on his shoulder and set out for the lake. The letter bid him be there in the evening, but because of its contents, Louis wanted to scout the shoreline one final time. He was familiar with the lake and surrounding terrain, but the water was wide and he had never hunted near the king's small castle, Berg.

Louis had received two other letters from the king since

that night, both vague and rambling essays on the purity of love and the evils of politics, of how Ludwig wanted nothing more than to follow his dreams in peace. Louis could respond to neither of them. All he could do was wait for the king to plan their next meeting and finally Ludwig had done it.

Louis was so nervous he could hardly hold his rifle steady. He doubted he'd catch anything this morning. What the king had asked involved real danger and no explanation was included. Louis's fingers touched the broken seal. Ludwig loved him, he reassured himself. He had to trust his king.

The lake was still, but not silent. It never was. In the trees the birds were calling and a wind blew rippling waves onto the shore. Louis skipped a rock across the surface as his eyes fell upon the king's lakeside home, south of Louis' own. He wondered what Ludwig was doing now, or if he was even yet there.

Chapter 24

Katza found Thekla in the kitchen.

"Thekla, what are you doing out of bed so early?" She saw the look on Thekla's face and knelt down beside her. "What is it?"

Thekla burst into tears. "I had a bad dream," she wept into her sister's arms.

"Hush now. Everything is fine."

"No. It isn't." Thekla sniffed as she tried to pull herself together. "I asked Louis to stay with me and tell me a story, but he wouldn't. He left."

"He'll be back," Katza said as she smoothed Thekla's hair. Even at her Thekla's young age, the years of fussing over her smaller sisters had hardened her to her own hurts.

Katza began to feel queasy as her vision blurred. She Saw the lake pouring into the kitchen and held on to Thekla to steady herself. Thekla, who knew her sister was prone to these moments, wrapped her arms tightly around Katza. Though Katza was her elder, Thekla acted as though she was the stronger of the two. Katza rose unsteadily, pulling free from Thekla's embrace. She left the kitchen without saying a word, leaving Thekla behind her.

Katza went to her room, where she sat on her bed and cried. It seemed as though a vision was caught behind her eyes and in its struggle to break free, every muscle in her face was being shred into pieces. It had never happened this way before. Katza was worried.

Her mother called them *spells*, but this was no magic. Katza could not control this unwelcome gift. It opened up moments in which the future appeared, often in amazing detail. It made her dizzy, but there was usually little more discomfort than that. Her Sight came when it would, but her visions were as reliable as clockwork. Everything she saw came to pass. Katza knew she ought to be seeing something now—it was there, just out of reach. She had to lie down before she was ill.

The moment passed without revealing a vision and left her with a feeling that something was horribly wrong. The whole morning was wrong; Thekla was not prone to nightmares and Louis, who did often go hunting in the early hours, would usually stay home if asked. It wasn't as though they relied on the game he caught. She suspected he used it as an excuse to explore the countryside. She had other suspicions, too, about his outings.

Katza had to somehow salvage the day. It was her birthday, after all, and she didn't want everyone out of sorts. Perhaps Louis would agree to an early picnic when he returned. She would invite Thekla, she suddenly thought. The girl was turning into an old maid right before their eyes. Katza could not understand why Thekla concerned herself so with their younger siblings. They already had a perfectly good, caring mother of their own.

The only time Thekla ever seemed happy was when she was at the piano, eyes closed tight, fingers on the ivory keys, but those moments were too few and too far between. Katza nodded to herself. Yes, her idea would help them all.

Katza waited for Louis in the hallway and greeted him when he came home.

"Good morning, Louis."

"And to you, Katza." He leaned down and placed a kiss upon her cheek. "How are you on this fine day?"

Her eyes narrowed. "I am well. Did you have any success this morning?"

"No, nothing today. There was a fog on the lake. I could hardly see to walk, much less to shoot."

"Ah." She chose her next words carefully. Sometimes the tiniest thing upset him. "You seem distracted this morning, Louis. Is everything all right?"

"Yes, everything is fine. Why do you ask?" She noticed how his hand fluttered over his pocket as he smiled.

"I thought we might have a picnic. Thekla had a difficult night and I'd like to do something nice for her."

Louis nodded. "She found me in the kitchen this morning. Something about dragons chasing her in her sleep. Are you sure you don't mind? You have to prepare for your party."

"That is hours away yet. I'll tell Cook to fix us a basket." She watched her brother's face. Something was going on and she was determined to find it out.

The three met later that morning by the kitchen door where Cook handed them a basket. Katza watched as Louis lifted the lid to inhale the scent of warm bread. She saw him draw a single rose from out of his sleeve and place it under the loaf.

The uneasy feeling that had been with Katza all morning crept closer to the surface of her skin. She shook it off and smiled as Thekla pulled her by the sleeve.

"Let's go." Thekla was impatient.

Louis and Katza linked their arms in hers and sang an old nursery song as they strolled out of the wide, front doors and into the world beyond, where Thekla spun out her joy on the grass.

They reached their destination in no time, a small hill overlooking the lake. It was calm, a pleasant surprise after all the rain they'd been having, though storm clouds were forming over the Alps. It would probably rain again and very soon.

Katza made herself comfortable on the blanket and let her eyes roam the sky. Smaller, friendlier clouds fractured and came together and among them, the black speck of a bird circled far over the trees.

How nice it would be, Katza mused, to be a bird. She closed her eyes and imagined her wings stretched in the air, nothing above her and the land well below. She was blinded as the wind swept tears from her eyes. She was blind and she was free.

"Today is your birthday. Aren't you excited?" The usually quiet Thekla was tugging on Katza's hem where it sprawled over the blanket and onto the grass.

Katza opened her eyes and smiled. "Not as excited as you are, I think."

Katza would have been more interested in her party, had she not felt this thing beneath her breastbone, this sinister, sinking thing that should be a vision.

Louis was quiet, lost in his thoughts, but Thekla seemed glad for his presence. She kept near to them as they sat in silence, trying to fit herself into their circle.

"Are you sure you are well, Louis? You don't seem yourself today." Katza had to ask again.

"I am fine, thank you."

They daydreamed, ate their bread and cheese and then folded up the blanket when the clouds overhead began to rumble. Louis gave the rose to Thekla, who clutched it to her chest.

Katza sent Thekla off to her rooms when they returned to the house and followed Louis to his. He took off his coat and hung it on the back of a stout wooden chair. She sat sideways on it and let her fingers toy with the collar.

"What is going on? Do not say it is nothing. Tell me what it is." As she asked him the question, she realized she might not want to hear his answer. They had never again discussed what Louis had said to her that day, nor had she ever mentioned the night of the king's visit, as promised. She felt she had to now.

"It is the king, isn't it? Has he come here again?"

"Nothing has happened, Katza. I beg you to stay out of that business. You would not approve in any case."

She smoothed his coat absentmindedly, as though heeding his words. Louis sat on the edge of his bed and began to remove his boots.

Head bent, he did not see Katza slide two thin fingers into

the pocket of his jacket. She gently eased the piece of paper away from the fabric and unfolded it as Louis sat up. He saw what she was doing and snatched the paper from her hand.

"I asked you to stay out of my business. I thought you respected me, Katza. How could you do this?"

"Do what?" Katza was confused. Couldn't he tell how she felt about him? Unlike Louis' infatuation with the king, her love was real. She'd seen enough. The letter in his pocket was from Ludwig.

"Sneak into my personal belongings to read a letter meant for me."

"That letter is from the king and you are a fool." Katza spat out the words more ferociously than intended and could not call them back.

Louis shook his head in disgust. "Leave me alone. I am going out tonight, I must rest."

"What do you mean, going out? It is my birthday." Katza was shocked.

"Katza, he's asked for me. I must go to him."

CHAPTER 25

THE HARD WOOD BENEATH HER CHEEK PRESSED HELENA slowly into consciousness. She raised her head carefully, felt for a bump and sat up to the sound of falling glass. Pieces of mirror littered the floor; some slid down her back when she moved. A tiny god peered out of each sliver. She stretched eight parts in equal measure and each part had a name. She was victorious—with Kitty's gift, she could now feed every one. Helena rose from the floor, complete and utterly ravenous. Her hunger had increased a hundredfold.

She searched for the key. It meant something to her now and she wanted to keep it. Helena couldn't wait to see Thekla's face when she learned of this. She saw the key flicker in the glass beneath the tiny window, scooped it up, and clasped the chain around her neck. She left the secret room and took her first cautious step down into the dark stairwell, where the air was heavy and damp. She felt as though she were suffocating and put a hand to her chest. The door at the bottom of the steps was open and light fell onto the lower three stairs. Helena reached the bottom and peered out from behind the curtain concealing the door.

Kitty sat, much as she'd left her, eyes open and focused on

Thekla, who stood in front of her sister a few paces away. Eva had her hand on the doorknob; she must have just entered the room. Thekla had a terrible expression on her face—what Helena could see of it. She held a rifle and had aimed it at Kitty. An eerie stillness shrouded them; nothing moved, not even the air as Helena breathed rapidly in and out of her nose.

"This isn't funny," she said to them.

No one answered. It seemed the entire world had ground to a halt along with her aunts. The windows were dark; all signs of the storm that had been raging outside when she'd first spoken with Kitty had vanished. A scarf of silence wrapped around her throat and tightened; she could not even use her own voice. She listened, but the house seemed as though it was sleeping. She should have at least heard the guests at her party—that many people make a terrible noise. There was nothing, not a single sound.

Helena edged past Aunt Eva carefully and followed the patterned rug in the hall past endless doors, every one of them open. She crept into the ballroom and caught her breath. The guests were there, and the group of four musicians in the corner, heads tilted at their violins. Above her head the stars hung motionless; the light of the sun had stopped revolving and all of the windows were dark.

It is a wax museum, she thought, remembering the pictures she'd once seen in a magazine Aunt Zilli had given her. She'd begged to be taken to one, but as usual, the answer had been no. Her eyes fell upon the pile of presents; the wrapping glittered and teased her. Helena let her fingers trail along the edge of the table. The lace on it rippled as her long nails snagged in its delicate latticework. The gaily wrapped packages waited, ready to reveal their contents at the cut of a ribbon. She looked up at the galaxy suspended from the ceiling, down into the frozen forest of guests and remembered that she was whole.

Helena shed fear like a skin—it was no part of her—and walked through the crowd like a big cat on the prowl. She ducked under dancers' arms and laughed at old Herr Krieger, who was bent over the roast with a fork in his hand. She toyed with the idea of knocking him down, but it would only be funny if he were awake to bear the brunt of her laughter. The expression of greed on his face as he stared at the succulent meat was too much.

Her stomach growled. Helena starved in more ways than one, but she did not want the food on the table. The kitchen, she thought. That never changes.

Its door, too, was open wide. There was no sign of Hope, but Helena thought nothing of it. She was most likely still in the ballroom, weirdly frozen with the rest. Helena did not care enough to search. She spied a bowl of fruit on the table, reached for an apple and then stopped herself. Helena's hand wavered above its glistening surface as her hunger turned to disgust. She could not eat any of this, she realized. She did not trust the fruit, or anything else in the house. Fear or no, she could not deny that something was horribly wrong.

Her gifts were clanging like church bells, each hungrier than the last. She wished she could take a knife to their need and shave off the worst of it, for they made so much noise she could now hear none of them clearly. She wished to hear

Eva's voice, or even Thekla's—anything to disrupt the clamor inside her. The house was a tomb, bricked up around her, and everyone in it seemed dead. Helena put a hand on her belly as it rumbled again.

"Wait," she said to her hunger, "until I figure this out."

She did not turn on any lights that were off, nor did she let her hands stray to the banister as she climbed the stairs. Oddly, the doors on the second floor were all open, too, revealing the private spaces of the family for easy inspection. She wasn't interested in them, not yet. She wanted the comfort of her own, familiar room and the face that so seduced her. She'd left Louis unfurled on her pillow and needed to be sure he was still there. She had the power now to bring him to life and she wanted to use it.

That he was her uncle meant nothing to Helena. He was as distant as the house in which she'd been born, over there, across the ocean. No one would tell her his story. Eva claimed not to recall him, and while Kitty must remember her brother, she hadn't seemed eager to share. Helena had to know more about him. This, she felt, was the purpose to which she'd been born. Her eighth gift, now named and found, demanded his restoration.

Kitty might know how to use her gift, but some things did not rely on time for they were perfectly timeless. Hours may have passed her by, or days. Hope had no way to tell. The sky remained dark but her lamp beamed ever outward. Her joints stiffened with pain and the house groaned in sympathy as she shifted the stool across the floor.

There was no time and space closed in around her as all else fell away. The secret room turned on its axis. Hope reached for another sliver of glass and watched the mirror spread under her hand.

₧₧

Helena emerged from her room. She wondered briefly what time it was, but the tall clock in the hallway was stopped at six on the dot. She suspected every clock in the house had done the same. The second floor hall was empty and the doors to all of the bedrooms still stood wide open. She could easily have entered any one of her aunts' rooms, but she already knew what they held. None of them were as compelling, as unknown to her, as the attic. It was there she had found him; perhaps there she would learn more.

She climbed the stair softly, afraid to make sounds of her own. Louis beckoned, lured her upward. She imagined she saw him walking ahead of her, just out of reach.

She stopped at the top of the steps, bewildered. The rooms on the third floor had always been empty, but for a random bed, or a bureau, abandoned and dull. Now, from out of the very room she had peeked into while Eva had rested her legs,

CHAPTER 26

HELENA SAW ONLY TWO OPTIONS. SHE MUST EITHER WAKE Kitty and pry more information from her or search the house now, while she had the chance, to see what she could learn on her own. With hidden rooms and an undisturbed attic, the house was ripe for exploration. The doors were already all open and inviting.

Helena paused at the end of the hall where she caught a strange scent in the air. Her bedroom door was open, too, but beyond it the room was dark. It smelled like a fire was burning in the hearth, though it had not been used since the end of winter, some few months ago. Helena took a hesitant step into the room. Her bed, the wardrobe and the dressing table were all gone. Her vision blurred and for just a moment, a fire did seem to be lit. She forced her eyes to blink. There were ashes, blackened and charred bits of wood, but no flame. They didn't belong there, either. Her mouth hung open. Her sanctuary had been transformed.

She swiped at cobwebs and shuddered when they touched her skin. She saw a small table and a cot, both rotted and damp from the moist air that clung to her skin. A sparse chair tilted against the far wall and a wooden mantelpiece hung crookedly above the blackened hearth. Her mantel was made of marble.

Helena did not know what to do or how to react. Her mind worked in a fury of confusion, trying mightily to comprehend her circumstance. Perhaps I am dreaming, she chanced to think, but this was no dream and she knew it. She decided to go along with it, for the gift of her great intellect was completely in awe of the challenge.

Without warning, a sudden fire roared up in the hearth and then subsided into a calm blaze. The light bounced from the glass fronts of hundreds of photographs, each held inside a unique frame. Creations of stone, wood, pewter and brass, beveled and shaped like nothing she'd ever seen peeked out from every corner. Helena, enchanted, moved to the table and chose one of them at random.

She recognized the face immediately. It was one of her aunts, but this was no aging crone with a bun of snow. The cheekbones gave her away, as well as the eyes slanting towards the high brow. It was Aunt Elfrieda—a very young Elfrieda. Her pale hair rolled over her shoulders and a tight corset bound her bosom, pushing the tops of her breasts over the fabric like two small crescent moons. She reclined on a divan with a vicious smile on her face. Helena wondered at who had been on the other side of the lens. She could not imagine that smile on the Elfrieda she knew.

Disturbed, she put the picture down and turned to another. Made of wood and carved in the shape of a dragon, this one held a different aunt asleep within the ribbon of its tail. Here was stern Thekla—it could only be she. Even as an elderly crone she had hair unlike any other, thick with curls and grown down to her knees. In her old age she kept it in a long braid that she sometimes wrapped around her head like a turban, only then to complain of its weight. Helena remembered asking her once why, if it bothered her so much, Thekla didn't just cut it all off. Thekla had been mortified by the idea.

In the photograph Thekla slept, stretched out upon a bed of frothy linens, her limbs relaxed as they never were in life and her hair unbound. Again, this was not the woman Helena knew. She put the picture down and picked up yet another.

Inside the tall, stone frame she recognized Ingeburg's white hair. She never wore it any other way than loose, and laughed when her sisters accused her of hedonism with a sad shake of their heads. Helena was almost in awe of Aunt Ingeburg's hair; it was white as the purest linen and felt like cotton. In the photograph Ingeburg sat in a large chair smiling with pleasure at a white cat that curled beside her. One hand gently rested upon the feline's large head, while the other held her weight behind her back. It seemed the picture was more about the animal than it was the woman. The lighting illuminated the wonderfully shaped head of the creature while leaving Ingeburg in relative darkness.

None of them had ever mentioned this cat, not even Ingeburg, who must have loved it very much.

In a gem-encrusted frame stood Zilli, posed beside a flowering tree. Its limbs dropped over her shoulders in a careless embrace. She was smiling and waving and wearing a dress that hung to her ankles in graceful folds of fabric. There was something wrong with Zilli, too. None of her aunts were quite themselves in these pictures. It was as though they'd been taken through the warped lens of memory; the photographer knew what the women might have looked like, but not who they were.

She felt like that now. Behind each face were thoughts unknown to her, and dreams she could not touch. Her aunts had never spoken of their past, and any reminders of their previous life—except for those forgotten in the attic—had been taken out of the house.

Helena felt dislocated. Her aunts' lives streamed away down the river of history while she was a fish, flopping on shore. She touched the other frames. Some seemed to be moldering already, falling into moss and mulch. She reached for another and the gilding fell off in her hand.

The image was of a young man, but it was no photograph. She recognized his face immediately and was anchored to the present. It was their brother, though in this painting he seemed very sad. His mouth was drawn and his arms hung lifelessly at his sides. He stood in solitude, patiently waiting for the artist to lay down the final stroke.

Helena's heart pounded in her ears as she was drawn into his eyes. They locked onto her own and beckoned for her to come closer, as though he wanted to speak to her through time itself but could not make his voice heard. Her head spun and she had that same, sick feeling in her stomach as she'd had when she found the old painting in the attic. Her appetite roared in frustration.

She wanted to take the little painting with her, but wasn't sure she could. As she watched, the room started to fade, the flames died down and the wreckage of a place left to lonely decay returned. Life sang and seared her and the other gifts echoed its call. Louis' eyes were accusing.

"A little more time," she croaked. "I just need a little more time."

CHAPTER 27

HOPE WATCHED HELENA COME TOGETHER AS SHE GLUED fragments of glass into place. It was a dangerous puzzle and each tiny piece mattered. Hope clucked when she saw the bare curve of Helena's shoulder in one of the shards. She disapproved of the dress the girl had chosen. It was obvious by her frozen reflection that Helena had been a mere breath away from the mirror when it had fallen from the wall. Her arms were stretched out as she held on to the frame. When her face was restored, Hope paused.

It had been years ago, when Helena had still been a small child, that Thekla warned Hope about their ancestral power, the inheritance that allowed them to give their unusual gifts. "It comes over us during adolescence, much like certain other aggravations, and is just as easily noticed. Watch for it in Helena's face. If you see anything before I do, let me know right away. I must be the one to tell her what has happened," Thekla had said.

"My goodness," Hope said into the quiet room, "what pretty eyes she has."

The timing could not have been worse. There was no way to tell Thekla now that Helena's power had arrived. Hope tapped her finger on the mirror, lost in thought. Helena's eyes, once dark, were now as clear as the spring where Hope's mother had drawn water each day. She was the one who had taught Hope to see possible futures in each ripple she made on the surface. Hope's mother never used mirrors. "We should never trust them for magic," she had said. "They are too modern and far too easily broken." As usual, Mother had been right.

Mirrors are dangerous objects; they can easily open doors, though few ever choose to enter. The best thing to do when people slip through is to guide them back through the door. Hope didn't think that was possible in this instance. This mirror was broken. Even when pieced back together again, this door might never open again. Damn you, Kitty. Hope coughed in her sleeve. *What have you done with Helena?*

Death shall lead you back—Kitty had meant for this all along. That the monster had turned out to be Thekla was certainly a shock, but Kitty must have foreseen her own demise and the method of its achievement. Did she think to catapult her soul back in time by way of it?

Hope had once heard of magic like this and believed it a pile of rubbish. She thought now, perhaps I was wrong. Eva had prevented whatever death Kitty had hoped for, yet still, the door had been opened. Did Helena step into the past in Kitty's place?

Hope had too many questions. The past cannot be changed. This was, as any child could tell, an indisputable fact. Hope adjusted her stockings and laces. Kitty had bet her own life against this fact. Perhaps Kitty knew something they didn't. She did have the gift of time.

Kitty might know how to use her gift, but some things did not rely on time for they were perfectly timeless. Hours may have passed her by, or days. Hope had no way to tell. The sky remained dark but her lamp beamed ever outward. Her joints stiffened with pain and the house groaned in sympathy as she shifted the stool across the floor.

There was no time and space closed in around her as all else fell away. The secret room turned on its axis. Hope reached for another sliver of glass and watched the mirror spread under her hand.

ℰ ℜ

Helena emerged from her room. She wondered briefly what time it was, but the tall clock in the hallway was stopped at six on the dot. She suspected every clock in the house had done the same. The second floor hall was empty and the doors to all of the bedrooms still stood wide open. She could easily have entered any one of her aunts' rooms, but she already knew what they held. None of them were as compelling, as unknown to her, as the attic. It was there she had found him; perhaps there she would learn more.

She climbed the stair softly, afraid to make sounds of her own. Louis beckoned, lured her upward. She imagined she saw him walking ahead of her, just out of reach.

She stopped at the top of the steps, bewildered. The rooms on the third floor had always been empty, but for a random bed, or a bureau, abandoned and dull. Now, from out of the very room she had peeked into while Eva had rested her legs,

SLEEPING HELENA

a great wall of roses spread out into the hall. Vines the size of
her forearm created a barrier that covered the doorway. At the
sight of them Helena retched and doubled over. She felt Louis'
heartbeat as it pulsed through the briars; she was shivering
with need. She straightened and unsteadily approached.

There was nothing wrong with these roses, she thought,
except they should not be here. Helena pulled at a spiking
tendril and it snapped back into place with a hiss. She stepped
away and surveyed the thorns, calculating the risks.

Helena had the gift of death and would not hesitate to use
it, but the vines were too tough to kill with her bare hands.
Her gift of grace would serve just as well and be glad to be
used. It gave her a supple skeleton with which she could slide
in among the branches and out through the other side. Helena
slipped off her shoes and entered as carefully as she could;
grace sang and led her onward.

It was a slow, determined dance with the monstrous
growth and she pierced her hands on the thorns several times
as she pushed them away from her face. Helena eased her way
forward until with a last turn of her torso she spilled out onto
hard stone. She raised her head and found herself staring at a
small wooden door. Its brass handle was shaped like a sword
and it was closed.

Helena pulled on the handle and the door swung slowly
open, revealing a passage carved out of stone. Torches lined
the wall in sconces of iron. Their flames jumped as she passed
by. She could feel him ahead; her hunger reached out, a
serpent's tongue tasting the air.

The tunnel found its end in a small room, the same size

as the bedroom normally situated in this part of the house. Instead of a bed, a long marble table sat at its center with a candle burning at each end. Their light was reflected by the armor that lay in quiet repose between them. Inside of it, she knew, was Louis.

Helena took a deep breath. Nausea swept over her; she staggered and reached for his arm. The metal was cold beneath her palms. If she dared to look, she would see her own face reflected in its polished plates. She closed her eyes and felt her way to his shoulder, leaned her hip against the table for balance and threaded her fingers under his helm. His hair was damp and it wrapped around her hand as she searched for a grip. Heat coursed through her body as she rested her head on his chest.

She heaved herself up, grabbed the helmet, and slowly eased it off. His head nearly cracked against the table, but she caught it in the crook of her arm just before it hit. With him cradled so close, she cautiously opened her eyes. She felt a sudden, sharp pain that stung long after the initial shock passed.

He was dead, there was no mistaking it, but it seemed she could again hear him calling. She leaned over his face, put her ear to his mouth and then listened at his throat. The sound was not coming from him. Life sprang up and out of her pores; its arms wove into hers and held Louis to her, eager to be fed. Here, at last, was what she'd been longing for. She was a god, made to take life and now finally able to give it, but that was not why Helena bent her mouth to his. She didn't *need* to kiss him. It was only that he called to her so, and made her ache for him. She put all of her godlike power into a petal-soft kiss.

Louis lay, head drooping, as before.

She was stunned. All of the will she'd put into that kiss had done nothing but embarrass and confuse her. She was a god and yet she'd failed to restore him. The two did not agree. If she was one, the other must follow. For the first time in Helena's life, tears flooded her eyes. She needed him. He was right there and she could not revive him.

CHAPTER 28

TIME IS A FUNNY THING. IT SEEMS SIMPLE, AS LONG AS ONE follows its usual footpath through the ages. Look closely and see how the past loops around to become the future, spiraling out and in, ever away and toward the present. Hope sat back to inspect her handiwork as somewhere in the house a grandfather clock chimed crookedly, out of tune. The room reattached to the stairs and the guests in the ballroom waited for time to turn. The mirror was two thirds completed, but that was the easy part. Hope had left the smallest pieces for last.

The endless repetition of gluing together the bits of broken glass had roused Hope from her trance. Each movement the same, every pinch of tired muscle, as though she'd done this a hundred times over. Hope rubbed her knees and stretched.

There was dust in her hair; she unpinned her bun and let the coil fall over her shoulder. She scratched her temple and pulled a grey hair out with two of her pointed fingers. I must look a fright, she thought, and then laughed. Her appearance had never mattered. She'd not seen an accurate reflection of herself since Thekla had removed all the mirrors. Except this one, of course, and hadn't that been altogether convenient.

Hope grimaced at the shards still scattered over the floor. They waited patiently for her hand to put them into place. Hope moved one with her toe instead. Kitty had laid her plans well. Her magic must have required a glance in a mirror, but why? The soul has its own transport; it only requires a guide.

Hope shook her head. I must be getting old, she thought. What better way to reach into the past than eye to eye? Kitty, unable herself to look into the mirror at the necessary moment, had Helena do it instead.

Mirrors lead to places. Kitty had chosen a mirror through which to use her gift. Don't stand between two mirrors, Hope's mother used to say. Your spirit will be trapped between them forever. Hope glanced at Helena, caught in the glass. If the moment between past and present stood between two mirrors… *good heavens*. Where did that leave Helena, who had walked straight into the void? More importantly, who would feed her?

Kitty's gift was a complicated one. Helena could be any-where, or nowhere, but if Hope was right and there were two mirrors, they were all very likely trapped somehow in time. They would bounce back and forth between the mirrors unless someone broke them both.

Hope moved another stray shard with her foot. Helena had destroyed this one, by accident or design. There must be another mirror out there, back in the past, most likely the very same one. Hope sighed and reached for her glue. One puzzle was plenty for her and she'd best get to it. The riddle of Kitty's gift belonged to Helena, where or whenever she was.

CHAPTER 29

HELENA WENT BACK THROUGH THE COLD STONE TUNNEL until it ended where it began. It would have been a perilous maze, but the roses had vanished and she easily made her way back to the hall. Sorrow fled in the face of her hunger. She tried to feed it with reason.

Surely I didn't dance my way out of the womb, Helena lectured herself. I had to develop her muscles and learn how to crawl before I could even stand.

It had been the same with all of her gifts; she'd had to grow into them. What muscles did Kitty's require? The power to give life—it was so tantalizing, so delicious. She had to know how to taste it.

She did not stop in any other room, no matter how enticing its contents. The house was degrading before her eyes; carpets moved and doorways shifted and the windows were full of night. The attic was her goal and she would not let herself be distracted. She hoped it was the same room she remembered.

It was not.

Helena marveled at what spread out on either side of her in the long room. Gone were the open timbers and rafters, the birds, the boxes, the dust. The ceiling was clean and white and the walls were paneled with mirrors. They hung between strips of gold-painted molding and in them the light of a thousand candles endlessly repeated. The room itself was empty; a wide and inviting space reminded her that dance was starving, too.

She loped toward the center of the room and felt it begin to feast. Arms outstretched, she performed a perfect grand jeté, but as her feet hit the floor, the mirrors began to frost over. The room became cold and the flesh on her arms pimpled. She rubbed them and wished for the sweater Hope had made for her birthday. Hope would know what to do, she thought as her teeth began to chatter. Hope always knew what to do.

Slowly the chill passed and the mirrors regained their clarity. Helena's skin returned to its normal temperature, but her reflection did not reappear in any of the glass. Instead, she saw Kitty's face in each mirror. Kitty was a different age in each one.

The images of Kitty carried on with their business in front of the mirrors while Helena spied from behind them. Here was the information she craved. She forgot about the cold and the guests waiting downstairs, her aunts and their unreal predicament—all of it. She was lost in the private life of the woman whose gift meant everything.

There was no order to the images. Kitty was a child in one, being carried on the shoulders of a sturdy, laughing man. She was ancient in another; Helena moved closer and watched her gnarled fingers struggle to button a dress. Helena knew that dress. It was the one Kitty had worn to her party. Helena peered into the room in which Kitty stood, gazing into the mirror now that she'd managed the last button. Kitty smoothed her hair and frowned at herself, and then walked out of the mirror's range. It went blank. In another, Kitty was a young woman who sat in a darkened room crying. A young girl came in and spoke to her, then left her alone again.

The next mirror was far more interesting. Kitty was old, but not ancient. She sat in a comfortable room at a dressing table and pawed through a box until she pulled out a slender chain. Helena watched her slip a tiny key onto it and clasp it around her neck. Helena knew that key, too. It hung around her neck now. Kitty must have been planning for this for years.

In the following mirror Kitty was younger still, though she sat at the very same table. Nothing, it seemed, had ever changed much in Kitty's long life. Here she was reading a blue leather-bound book. The lines were faded, the script from another age. Helena put her face as close as she could to it and tried to make out the words.

It was some sort of list—wait, that was her name there, and the names of all of her aunts were written above it. She scanned through them quickly. It was a record of the gifts each one had been given; her eyes went immediately to Kitty's name just as she closed the book. *Time.* Kitty's gift was time. What an odd gift, Helena thought. How would you use it? The possibilities were endless, she mused. Kitty had obviously squandered her gift. Helena shook her head. She would not share her aunt's fate.

Helena moved aside. In the next mirror she saw Louis just as he leaned out of its range. She would have swooned with the usual vertigo, but the look on Kitty's face restored her balance.

She recognized her aunt's expression. It was hunger, raw and hurting, and it was turned away from Louis, as though Kitty did not want him to see it. In her aunt's face Helena saw her own need mirrored. It disturbed her more than any other mad thing that was happening.

Helena backed away and took a deep breath. She was weak and felt faint, and none of what she saw was helping. There were secrets here, she knew that much, but she was no longer certain she wanted to share them. Kitty became an immediate adversary. Helena found it did little good to remind herself that she was the only one of them who would have Louis. Helena was no better off than Kitty, not until she could use the gift Kitty had given to her.

Her eyes searched out one more mirror, the least revealing of all. In the others, there was movement, as though Helena were watching the scene as it unfolded. This mirror was more of a still life. Kitty was young, close to her own age, Helena guessed. Her back was to the mirror, but her face was turned toward it. Behind her a crowd blurred, but Kitty's shape was clear. She looked straight into Helena's eyes, but said nothing.

"How strange it must be to be caught like that, with nothing to see but yourself until someone frees you."

Helena didn't realize she was speaking out loud, but her voice jarred her back to her senses. She remembered her own face in the mirror and felt greed course through her blood. She had learned nothing new about Louis or of how to use her gift. It was time to get out of this room and go back downstairs.

It was a setback, but somewhere she'd find an answer. She

wished she knew where Kitty lived; she'd like to read that book from cover to cover and find out who had what. Her aunts could do more with their gifts, she thought, if only Thekla would let them. Thekla clung to power like a fragile caterpillar does to a shaking leaf. She probably knew something, too.

Helena left the attic. On the third floor, the roses were still gone, replaced by a door with nothing unusual about it except that it was closed. They were all closed now, but Helena paid no attention.

All the doors on the second floor were still open. She ignored all but the entrance to Thekla's room, walking directly to it. Inside, she let her eyes roam over Thekla's sparse belongings. Tension she did not know she was holding evaporated. The room was unchanged, a relief after everything she'd seen so far this evening.

She would have to admit it sooner or later. She was not going to find what she needed on her own. Her aunts had to be woken and made to share the wealth.

It was instinct that led Helena to Thekla's bedside table, an innocent piece of darkly carved wood with a doily placed neatly on top of it. Helena yanked its single drawer open. The usual pencils and paper, envelopes and lipsticks were all neatly ordered in front. Behind them was a flat silver box she'd never seen. Helena nudged it out of the drawer and flipped up the delicate latch.

Several items lay on a velvet cloth: a gold locket, a creased letter, and a flake of ivory from the top of a piano key. Helena set the box down and pulled out the locket. Its chain was thin and fragile and its clasp was tarnished, but it opened easily when she put her nail in the seam and wedged the two halves apart. On one side was a tiny portrait of Louis, on the other, a curl of dark hair. Helena paled at the sight and quickly closed it. She draped the chain around her neck, so the locket hung next to the key.

The letter was crumbling; pieces of brittle, yellowed paper fell away from the edges as Helena took it out of the box. The writing was almost illegible. She carefully smoothed out the creases and squinted her eyes at the words. It was addressed to Thekla and was only a few lines long.

"Do not cry, dear sister, for I have found a way to bring our brother back. Perhaps you will forgive my departure when I've reunited us all. Your sorrowful life will vanish, we shall be a family once more, and I promise, when all is done, not to leave you again. With love, Katza."

Katza. It had to be Kitty, but what did she mean, found a way? Maybe she hadn't squandered her gift after all. With a gift such as time, Kitty could erase the future. *But if she'd done it already, I would not be here,* Helena thought. Kitty was clearly lying to Thekla. They must have been playing games with each other for ages. Helena's thoughts were spinning; she tried to imagine a lifetime of this and failed. These women were utter strangers to her, every last one of them. Helena wanted her old aunts back, even Thekla, most secretive of all.

CHAPTER 30

THEKLA FORGOT ALL ABOUT HER NIGHTMARE. IN DREAMS the dragon slumbered on, leaving small girls undisturbed. Thekla held the rose Louis gave her, put it to her face and inhaled its scent. Her brother had been acting strangely for the last few months and she hadn't been sure what to make of it. Louis had drawn himself in, away from them all, as though he knew things but was unable to share them with those he loved. Today he was his usual self and her spirits were lifted because of it. There was also Katza's party to come, and Thekla was very excited about that.

Her new dress was spread out on the bed. Mama had it specially made for the party. It was of lilac silk with a matching lace jacket, not like the child's clothes she was usually forced to wear. A proper dress for a proper young lady, Mama had said, and Thekla felt as though she were finally growing up. Since she was now a young lady, Louis would ask her to dance. She was very much looking forward to that moment. She touched the silk of her dress carefully, ran a finger over the collar and saw herself wearing it as she was twirled through the ballroom on her brother's strong arm. Her joyous reverie was broken when she heard a door slam shut in the hall.

Thekla peeked out to see what was happening. Though the

hallway was empty, she thought she could hear someone sobbing behind Katza's closed door. Dress forgotten, Thekla tiptoed toward her sister's room.

It was crying, and it sounded like Katza. Thekla could not understand it. This was Katza's birthday—she should be happy. She seemed fine at the picnic, though she had lied to Louis about her earlier fit. Maybe she was having another one.

Thekla pushed on the door to see if it would open. It did and she took a cautious step into the room. She risked Katza's anger at the intrusion, but Thekla didn't like to think of her sister in pain. Katza was huddled in a chair by the window, face in her hands, shoulders shaking.

"Katza, what is wrong? Are you having a headache?" Sometimes her sister's head hurt because of her spells, Mama said, but she'd never seen Katza like this. "Katza?"

Katza raised her head. Tear-blurred and reddened eyes focused on Thekla, who fiddled with a string fallen loose from a button while she waited for her sister to speak.

"What do you want?" she finally said, her voice sharp and bitter. It was obvious that Katza was not well.

"I want to know what's wrong." It seemed simple to her. Why else would she be here?

"Nothing is wrong. Go away."

She should do as her sister asked and leave her alone, Thekla thought, but that was not Thekla's way.

"I won't go until you tell me why you are crying," she said to Katza, who had put her head back down and hid her face from sight.

"You're too young to understand," Katza mumbled.

Thekla hated that. She was not too young. Didn't her new dress prove it? She could handle Katza's problems. She was a young lady now, too.

"I am not," she said defiantly.

℘℧

Katza opened an eye and looked at her sister; she'd never spoken to her like that before.

Nothing was going right today; even the picnic had been a complete disaster. Thekla had received a rose Katza knew was meant for Ludwig. Louis could not keep his eyes away from the lake. Thekla *was* too young, she could not know how it felt to have one's love scorned by another, even if the love is that of a brother.

There would never be anyone but Louis, not for Katza. Louis was her champion and her only hero. He had cared for her while she was blind, and then taught her how to see the world with her newly opened eyes.

Louis had betrayed that bond by falling in love with another. Katza's heart was broken.

Katza craved the past. This was a small seed, not yet the rose that would pierce the rest of her life with its thorns, but it was a beginning. She wished to return to the days when Louis championed her—only her and no other.

She had such longings; she did not know what to do with them, where to land them, where to begin the quest to fulfill them. She thought of the bird in the clouds and blamed her own broken wings on Ludwig.

Katza was a dark cauldron. Jealousy bubbled and a foul potion began to brew.

"It is only that my head hurts." Katza spoke as kindly as her hoarse throat would allow. "I'll be fine. You return to whatever you were doing." Katza smoothed her hair away from her forehead as if to say, see, I am putting myself back together. Don't worry about me.

"Are you sure? Would you like something to drink?" Thekla was more than willing to travel down to the kitchen and back, if it would make her sister feel better.

Katza, exhausted, let her mask slip. "Go on, go away," she said as she rested her head on the edge of the chair.

Katza could not tell Thekla about the way a vision pressed at her eyelids, that a monster was there, waiting for its chance to gobble them all up. She may as well be blind, for all she was able to see it. She would frighten Thekla, and the girl was just trying to help.

₱₱

Thekla backed away from her sister and slipped out of the room. She closed the door quietly behind her, leaned against it and let out her breath. Just that morning her sister had treated her kindly and now she acted like a beast. The dragon raised its wide, flat head. Thekla shivered.

Mama came up the stairs just then and found her.

"What is the matter, my dear?"

"Katza was crying. I tried to help her, but she told me to go away." Thekla wiped her eye with a fist as her lips trembled.

"Never mind, she'll come around. We have to leave her in peace when she has her spells."

Katza always comes first, Thekla thought. Even now she's allowed her moment, while I have to be strong.

CHAPTER 31

LOUIS REACHED THE FIRST FLOOR IN TIME TO SEE BARONESS von Tress with her pinched face and sharp tongue being escorted into the library. A friend of the family, she'd been invited to Katza's party. She was not expected until later. Louis didn't much care for the old Baroness, though it was she who first sparked his interest in Ludwig with her wild tales and gossip. She was a very close friend of the king's.

They were trying times for Ludwig, but Louis was sheltered from much of the truth simply because he lacked interest in it. Louis lived by his heart, and now from within its impenetrable walls it told him, *something is wrong*. The Baroness should not be here, and she should certainly not be entering the library. That was his father's domain.

Louis' vision expanded, the letter in his pocket demanded he pay attention. He caught Magdalena as she hurried into the hall.

"The Baroness is here. Do you know why?" Louis held his mother's arm firmly. He was a man now, with a man's desire to know of the happenings in the house.

"No, I do not." She gently removed her son's hand from her elbow. "I've just been called down from the nursery. You are welcome to join us, though if asked to leave, you must do so immediately and without complaint. Papa will insist."

Louis deflated in front of his mother. He nodded his assent. He might be a man, but it was still his father's house.

As they entered the library the scent of tobacco from Papa's pipe closed in around them. The high-ceilinged room was lit with lamps, for just after midday the clouds had reformed. It would storm again that night. Louis settled his thoughts on the Baroness, who sat primly on the edge of a chair. She turned her bird's eye on him and inclined her chin. He had permission to stay.

"I will not spread gossip here," she said firmly. "This is the truth; I have seen it myself. Ludwig is in great danger. They must have him in the asylum by now."

Louis hardly heard his father's response. "Who has taken him? What do you mean?"

"That idiot doctor and his apostles, that's who I mean. It is all lies!" She banged the tip of her parasol on the floor. "They have declared Ludwig insane and are having him deposed. I tried to warn him of this, but it was too late. They have intercepted all of his messages and are holding him hostage at Berg, I am sure of it. He was removed from Hohenschwangau early yesterday morning. My informants tell me they were headed this way. I must do something to help him!"

It was at Berg that Ludwig had told Louis he'd meet him, after the other business was done. Ludwig must have somehow sent the message, but for whatever reason, he had left out certain details. Possibly important details, but it made no difference to Louis. He was a knight who would go gladly to his king's rescue.

"Why are you telling us this?" Papa's interest in his king was that of a subject rather than a friend. "What can we do?"

"I wish to stay here for a time nothing more. I will not involve you in anything I may or may not do while I am a guest in your house."

Mama spoke. "Baroness, you are more than welcome to remain here as long as you like." This was Magdalena's realm. "We are a humble family, as you know, but will do our best to provide for your needs."

"There is little humble about your family, Magdalena." The Baroness smiled knowingly and tightened her grip on her parasol. "I'll hear none of it. It will be my pleasure to stay. Thank you for having me."

The household absorbed its noble guest like any other. A set of rooms on the third floor was aired out and made ready while the Baroness chatted about the children and other innocent things. Katza's party should go on as planned, of course. It was not her intent, she said, to disrupt their lives. She could not know how her words affected Louis.

He made his excuses and left Mama and the Baroness talking quietly about other affairs and made his way to the stable. The horses jumped anxiously at the approaching storm and the grooms were out in force, trying to calm them. Louis stroked his favorite mare absentmindedly.

There had been a time when Louis had all he needed in his sister's circumstance. As blind Katza had regained her sight and become self-reliant, Louis, cut adrift, had reached out for a new cause. He'd found an icon in tales of the Magic King, and love in the man himself.

Now Ludwig had a real need of him and Louis, a natural champion, felt restored to his purpose.

He was sorry the king had arranged the meeting on the night of Katza's party, but there was nothing he could do about that. This was a chance that would only come once in a lifetime. His sister, he believed, would be fine without him.

ఴ ౪

Katza's anger kept her pinned to her chair as the minutes ticked by on the brass clock beside her bed. Louis was going to meet the king and there was nothing she could do to stop him. The vision beat at the back of her eyes and every muscle in her body tensed with the knowledge that some terrible thing was coming. All she could do was rage at her brother for wanting to spend time with the king. It was wrong of Louis to do this to her.

A bird sang in the window; she took off her shoe and threw it. The bird flew off, but its presence had Katza out of the chair. As she pulled the shutters closed, she noticed the storm returning. She wanted the rain to keep Louis inside, but there was no hope for it. Even this wouldn't keep him from meeting his make-believe lover.

She no longer cared about her party. It was something to endure, nothing more. If she had anything to do with it, she'd call the whole thing off. She would smile for her guests, but would get no enjoyment herself out of the evening.

178

By the time the guests began to arrive, she was dressed and ready to greet them. Her mood was unchanged and she did not try to hide it. Katza no longer cared if her parents discovered her brother's secret. She almost hoped they would—maybe that would make him stay. She aimed her displeasure at him. She wanted Louis to feel as horrible as she did.

The party began slowly as more guests were absorbed into the ballroom, where a feast waited to be eaten and a small group of musicians played. The Baroness was doting but distracted. Katza paid her little heed. Her parents' eccentric friend moved off into the crowd as Katza found a corner from which she could watch for Louis. He was late and she was worried.

She saw Thekla in the crowd, but hardly noticed how pretty her sister looked in her lovely new dress. She followed Thekla's eyes and found Louis. He was speaking with their father at the far end of the room. Katza made her way through polite handshakes and kisses, greetings and well-wishes, short speeches and plates of food being pressed upon her until she came out in a clearing near the table.

Louis was avoiding her; he slid through the crowd until he reached Thekla's side, where he leaned his face down to her cheek. He straightened and looked Katza in the eye, smiled wanly and raised his glass.

Mama said something, but Katza barely heard her. Katza kept her eyes on Louis. Some small part of her felt she could still intercept him. It was early, just six o'clock, and anything could yet happen.

Someone brushed against Katza's shoulder. Without thinking, she turned to move out of their way. As she did, she caught her own reflection in a mirror on the opposite wall. But it wasn't her—Katza's blue eyes met grey, her blonde hair was black, and the face was that of a stranger. Katza blinked in surprise. When she opened her eyes, her own face appeared, as it should.

Katza shook the strange vision away, turned back toward the ballroom, and searched the crowd for Louis. He was gone. She bolted. Katza pushed her way through the guests and ran to the kitchen, where Cook was overseeing the delivery of more wine to the ballroom. She darted among the staff and out into the garden and was immediately drenched by the pouring rain.

Katza ran through the garden and its pergola, only stopping to flail at the vines that tangled over her head. She reached the courtyard, heard Louis' horse at the stable and darted over the flagstones. She was determined to catch him, but the ground was wet and Katza lost her balance. Her hair blew into her eyes and she slipped, one foot twisting under the other. She fell. Her head cracked on a stone. She lay still on the cold ground, blooding mingling with rain around her as Louis leapt astride his horse and rode away.

CHAPTER 32

THEKLA'S BEDROOM REVEALED NO FURTHER SECRETS AND when Helena finally left it, the other doors were closed. She was sure hours had passed; she simply had to eat something. The kitchen beckoned. She could almost smell a fresh loaf of bread being pulled from the oven. Maybe Hope is awake, she thought, and baking something as usual.

On the first floor of the house, the doors to the ballroom hung open on heavy, gilded hinges. Helena expected to find her guests just as she'd left them, but the whole house had changed while she'd been exploring upstairs. A huge chandelier hung from the center of the ceiling; tiny flames were caught mid-flicker on hundreds of wicks. The walls were lined with heavy paintings and mirrors, Rococo monstrosities that could not possibly bear their own weight, yet somehow did. The ladies wore dresses with billowing skirts and immense jewels upon their gloved fingers. The men sported long jackets and trousers, gruff sideburns and gold pocket watches. It was a party, but these guests had not come for her. She saw the table at the far end of the room, just where she'd left it, and on it a large pile of wrapped presents. Everyone was still.

Helena finally began to lose her bearings. She drifted through the crowd like a lonely, windswept leaf among unmoving trees. She began to think it *was* her party—if she looked closely enough she would see Herr Krieger, happily eating the roast. She moved and whirled and stepped through the guests as though they were all watching. She lost herself in a small revelry. In her mind the music played and she was singing. She knocked into a burly man with a curling moustache and halted in place, kept still as the rest of them and listened for any sound. He did not respond; no surprise showed in his expression.

The far table, covered with glittering paper and ribbons and unopened boxes, drew her attention. Helena, dazed, walked toward it. As she did, her eyes fell on a young girl's face.

"I know her," she said out loud, her voice entering the silent room like a thief. "Aunt Thekla?" *What a pretty dress,* Helena thought. *So light.*

Helena recognized the lines on Thekla's face. She knew them hardened by age, but they were there now, soft as snow, already. How sad, to be so young and yet so full of sorrow. It felt odd to have such thoughts about another; compassion was no part of Helena, but as it arrived and unpacked its luggage, she unthinkingly made a place for it. The ballroom cast a strange shadow over Helena, the dancers beckoned and their eyes gleamed while Helena felt like stone.

She seemed very large compared to Thekla. It was discouraging to think that this fragile child would become one of her creators. She turned and saw another face across the expanse of the room.

"There I am again, frozen like everyone else," she said at her reflection. She *was* frozen, and if she didn't do something, she would become like the people around her. Still weakened by hunger and burning with need, the fugue vanished at the sight of her face in the mirror. She looked like a ghost in a torn and dirty red dress. She had to get out of the house.

Helena shook herself out of the mirror, left the ballroom undisturbed and went through the small door at the back of the room. She was famished, her stomach grumbled and her gifts cried out for attention. She wished she'd find Hope in the kitchen, alive and well. Hope would know what to do. That was the thing about Hope that most disturbed her. Hope always knew what to do and was always there to do it. It was an unexpected love she felt for Hope as she crept through the silent house, but again a place within her was created for it. Though made of eight parts and not one thing more, Helena was somehow expanding.

In the hall candles were trapped in their guttering. The carpet was patterned with roses and the wood was dark and warm. Mirrors hung on the wall in a row, each more ornate than its neighbor. Helena could not resist a glance into every one of them. *This is what they think beauty looks like,* she thought of her aunts, or at least whichever one of them had given it to her. Elfrieda, most likely. She was the sweetest of all. Helena was entranced by the sight her image. She'd gone most of her life without clearly seeing it and her face was a curious surprise.

She remembered the day Aunt Thekla had the mirrors removed. She must have known even then what Kitty's gift was and had planned to keep Helena from finding it. Helena faced it; her mantra rang in her ears. *They knew.*

It really had been going on for years.

"What then," she paused to ask, "does that make me?"

Did they create her to have something new to fight over?

Some pieces of Helena sloughed off, others rearranged. She was a god who was not a god. Her makers were a bunch of old ladies and yet, they *had* created her. It nagged at her, yet she had no word for what she was feeling. Debt was nothing she understood, yet now it seemed she had one.

They had known all along. They had made her up out of their gifts and then they hid one of those gifts from her. Anger slid down her spine like drops of water, it splashed on the floor at her feet and muddied her hem.

They made her. It didn't really matter why they'd done it. Helena owed her life to these women. Is this where gods find themselves at the end?

She reached the kitchen, where she hoped what she knew to be true would be reinforced. This was her house. That was her kitchen, where every day Hope cooked her meals. The air stank of roses. Hope would not like this, she thought, but Hope was not there to see it.

The shape of the room was the same. That was all Helena recognized of Hope's comfortable domain. There were plates of food and barrels of beer and was that a dog in the corner? There were several young maids and a fat cook, and a butler behind him holding a tray of pastries. Helena's stomach rumbled to remind her that she had not yet eaten. She had come here for food, but no. She turned her back on the scene. She could not bear it.

She left through the door to the garden, where light from the many windows spilled into an early evening darkened by storm clouds. She stopped in amazement. Across the walls draped a wave of roses, like a red curtain over the stones. Their stems were healthy and green and buds glistened with raindrops that studded their spiraling petals. They were nothing like the surly briars Helena knew, but if she peered at the roses from the corner of her eye, it looked as though the others were there, stretching just beneath them.

The air was still; the roses did not waver and around her Helena began to notice more things out of place. Where Hope had planted mint, onions now grew. What should be a path was the mint patch. And the cabbages! They grew in a row by the wall. Everything was there, but none of it was where it belonged. Helena began to feel sick. She put a hand on her stomach, looked down and shook her head at the state of her once lovely dress.

The door into the kitchen glowered, it seemed, and dared her to return through it. The basil was where the fountain should be and the fountain was near the bench. The bench was beside the arbor, but the door to the house was the same. She knew what waited inside. She'd hoped things would be different out here, but apparently she was wrong. She began to panic; she sped through the garden as shadows lurched from the vegetable patch and clematis tugged at her hair. The rose bushes scrabbled over the stone and the great house was a menacing moon hanging over her shoulders.

She reached the far wall and the arched doorway that led through it. Helena stopped at the door; it seemed familiar though she was certain she'd never noticed it before. Beyond it, a pergola dripped with sodden vines. She darted into its sheltering framework and scrambled through it, finally reaching the courtyard where she slowed, out of breath. The scent of wet hay and clover filled the air, fresh and sweet. Helena could take little more. The whole world was frozen. She felt like the only person walking on earth.

She crouched by the wall. Her eyes frantically roamed the courtyard as she looked for a sign of life. There was none, just the trees beyond the flagstones and the buildings at the far end. She shifted her position and spied a shape sprawled out on the ground in front of the stable.

This is my house, Helena reminded herself. *This must be my courtyard*, she thought, even though she'd never seen it before.

She crossed the stones and knelt down beside the figure. It was Aunt Kitty, sublimely young and immobilized. She did not feel like the others. As far as Helena could tell, Kitty was not frozen. She was dead. How had she signed her letter?

Katza.

This is not my time, Helena realized as she looked upon the fallen body of her aunt. It explained why the guests' clothing was so strange, why the maids in the kitchen wore skirts to the floor and why there was a dog by the hearth.

It was impossible.

Helena peered around the courtyard to see whether anything else was amiss. The vertigo engulfed her and the familiar waves of nausea rocked through her body. By the stable she saw another figure. She knew who it was.

The outline of a horse took shape in the shadow of the

stable. On it sat a single rider. He and the horse faced away from the stable, as though they were riding out into the forest. It had been storming when Helena had found the mirror. He had obviously been caught in a storm, too. His coat was drenched with water, though not one drop fell from his sleeves. Helena carefully circled the beast. She could hardly stand upright. The horse's muscles were clenched as though he was preparing to leap toward the wood when he and his rider were stopped. Helena's eyes moved from the horse to the man, she followed the trail of his thigh up to his face. It was Louis. He was trapped, like all the others, but he was alive.

CHAPTER 33

HELENA WAS COLD AND TIRED. SHE COULD NOT, NO MATTER how she craved him, remain so close to Louis. Her hunger was too great.

She crept back to the garden wall, crouched in the weeds and stared blindly at the stable where horses stood, heads bent to their feed, with grooms poised just beside them. This was her house, but not her time. She was a hundred years early to her own party, or a hundred too late to this one. She cared for neither party now. She just wanted to go home and somehow take Louis with her.

"I must have come through the mirror," she said to no one, "for as soon as I got Kitty's gift, everything changed."

The mirror, she recalled, was broken. Could she still get back? She looked at the house and the windows facing the courtyard. Shadows cast a strange patina on the brick. Inside the light never flickered.

The mirror might be there now, on the wall, just as it was in the future Helena remembered. But Louis was here, in the past, and he was alive. Helena had only to wake him. Her gift howled. Perhaps Kitty had sent Helena back in time to save him—Kitty did have the gift.

Helena frowned and scratched at her ankle. She should go back in and see if the mirror she came through was there in that secret room. She shuddered. She could not face the sight of those people, still as statues, not breathing, and yet not dead.

Helena rose, unsteadily, and circled the garden without entering it. The wall met the side of the house halfway to its front. Beyond it, the lawns spread out like a bed, large enough for a giant, soft enough for a frail princess who might feel the smallest pebble beneath her hip. Trees twisted against the grey sky, their shadow-flung arms open wide to catch the light emanating from the windows of the house. The ground declined toward the lake, rimmed with a black shade of reeds. Helena was drawn to the water as though it was Hope, calling her in for supper.

Helena suddenly found herself grateful for Hope's steady presence. Hope had taught her so much without saying a word, though Helena was only now coming to see it. Love did not sit well with Helena, but it was an insistent guest and seemed determined to stay.

She put all thoughts of Hope out of her mind. Hope could not help her now. She made her way to the shore of the lake, the grounds left behind without further notice. She was too busy ordering her thoughts. The house had disoriented her, but the fresh air was restoring Helena's balance. Louis was there and he was alive. Somehow he had to be woken. Helena needed answers, but only Katza had them. In this state, she did not see how she'd be able to rouse any one of them.

Helena did not think of Louis as another girl might. He

was no handsome young man whose attention she desired. Instead, every bit of her rose up to his song, as though he was what all eight gifts craved and what she'd fed them so far was a morsel. The song was so sweet as to be sickening. She had to have him, had to make him her own. She looked up. The shore was before her.

There were waves on the lake, the first sign of movement she'd seen outside of the house. Her relief was overpowering. An old twisted tree grew beside the water. A wooden swing had been tied to one of its outstretched limbs. She wondered how it would feel to propel herself up and wing away like a bird. A silly thought, but she was weak and the seat looked inviting. She rested her legs; the ropes held her weight. Helena swung as the waves gently spread on the shore. If she closed her eyes, she could almost imagine she was flying.

Air rushed past her face as she swung even higher. It was so good to feel something move alongside her; not one breath had stirred the air inside the house. She had no idea how much time had passed since she'd woken to find the mirror smashed around her, or if time had passed at all.

It had been a beautiful mirror—the only one privileged enough to remain in the house when Thekla had banned all the others—and then she had come along and destroyed it. She hadn't meant to break it; remorse knocked on the door at the thought. Helena shook her head and pumped her legs even harder. She would not hear such thoughts. They were not of her, but despite her denial, remorse found a crevice in heart and there it stayed.

She could have danced in the still night, or sang to the

cloud-covered stars, or offered a simple smile were she at home. All would be resolved around her; it was a gift. Eight gifts, she thought, most of them useless now. Helena recalled the way Aunt Thekla's face only softened when she heard music. Thekla must have given me music, she mused. The twins, of course, were of song and dance, and Zilli's gift had to be grace. Ingeburg, witty and clever, must have given her intelligence.

That left Eva and Kitty, but which of the two had given her the gift of death?

She'd believed all along that Kitty's gift had been life, which left Eva to have given her death. But that made no sense at all, not as she now understood it. The others had given something of themselves, but there was no hint of death in Eva. Kitty was the one who stank of that.

Helena brought the swing slowly to a halt. She had figured this out years ago but never made the connection. Life and death were inseparable. She turned eight parts around in her mind and inspected each one as best as she could. If Kitty's gift was death, life went with it, which meant that Eva's gift of life had been there all along—as had been Kitty's. If that was the case, what did her aunts think they had been hiding? The lake before her offered no ready answer.

Helena's mind worked in a fury. She was thrown back to those childish days when her eighth part had plagued her, and finding its name had been all that mattered. She remembered her face in the mirror. It could not now be denied that she was, in fact, complete—the difference in her was obvious. The new additions, those emotions that

191

crept in through the door when she wasn't paying attention, reminded her of their presence.

I am more than complete, she thought. The swing began to rock again as her legs pushed her back and forth of their own volition.

She let the swing's movements lull her. She listened to the rustle of the rushes as they washed to and fro in the waves lapping the shore. As she watched the ripples on the water, a strange vision parted the fog in the center of the lake. A large, red swan pulled a boat with a prow made of golden filigree toward the shore. Helena's stomach lurched, the swing twisted and she spun around. She clung to the coarse ropes as though they were her only tethers to sanity. There was a man at the helm, his bulk mantled in moonlight, standing as motionless as the guests at the party. A *V* of waves spread open behind the swan as it swept silently toward her across the water. The palms of her hands were scraped raw and her strength fled. Helena slid to the ground, ill and feverish, as her gifts began to shriek.

CHAPTER 34

THE GRASS WAS COOL AGAINST HELENA'S CHEEK. SHE watched from an angle as the little craft stopped at the shore. The swan flapped away from the water and the man climbed out of the boat. His boots filled her vision; they had no eyelets to count. He was dressed in kingly garb and bore himself proudly, despite the odd method of his arrival. The swan stretched its great wings and then settled and turned its head to the side. Its black eye looked directly at Helena. Her body violently reacted; she coughed and spit on the ground.

The man reached his hand out to Helena as she gazed up at him with reddened eyes. His smile somehow calmed her. She took his hand and felt strength flow through her body. She climbed to her feet with ease.

"You do not belong here," he said.

"I could say the same about you."

A burst of laughter erupted from him. "I live here, Helena, though you are correct. This is not my home."

"How do you know my name?" Helena felt like her old self again, though her gifts were unusually silent and only moved listlessly inside her.

He answered her questions by asking another. "Do you know where you are?" He looked down on her kindly, a patient teacher in front of a potentially difficult student.

Helena wanted to say *beside the lake*, but somehow she could not bring herself to treat him as she had her tutors. He imposed his presence upon her as they never did and he expected an answer in honesty.

"No. Not really. I think I've gone back in time." She had to admit it.

Maybe he could help her get out of this place, or knew how she could bring it to life.

The man smiled, but it was more of a child's grin. "This is my land and I was king of it, but it is no land as you understand it."

"You are mad."

"So it is said." He did not seem disturbed by her accusation.

Helena found something familiar about him; she checked her memory for clues. It could take time for less important things to surface from her vast store of knowledge, but she finally placed him and practically in her own garden.

"You're Ludwig the Second," she said. "I've seen pictures of you."

The king nodded. "I am more the memory of Ludwig, but yes, that is my name."

"Where am I?" She was unimpressed by royalty. If he had any answers, she wanted to know them.

"You have not gone back in time, as you think. You have entered into memory. Here time stands still."

His words confused Helena. "Memory? Whose memory?"

"It belongs to a woman named Katza. I think you might know who I mean."

"My aunt? How do you know Kitty?"

"I've known her many times over," he said, which only confused Helena more. "She remembers what she will of me. I've been here for many long years."

Helena did not like contradictions. "If time does not flow here, how can you measure it?"

"It is measured by Katza's life."

The stories were right; he was out of his mind. She didn't have time for this. "How do we get out?"

"One of you must wake."

"Wake?" Helena was not sleeping.

"You or Katza must wake into time. Both of you may not. You must make the choice that Katza cannot."

She thought of the tomb-like house and the guests, trapped in both past and future, and of Louis, who was so close she could almost taste him. Helena's forehead creased as she puzzled this out.

"If only one of us can wake, what happens to the other?"

That king said nothing as within Helena, death begged for satisfaction. Helena found herself suddenly unwilling to feed that particular gift. She did not like ultimatums, but suspected the king was right; she had no reason not to believe him. One of them must wake or none of them would, not even Louis.

She considered each of Kitty's possible futures. Helena needed no special sight to predict what would happen should she awake in front of the mirror she had broken. She saw Thekla aiming the rifle, clear as glass, at Kitty, who would die within seconds of Thekla pulling the trigger. Helena saw, too, the cold body on the flagstones. Here and now Katza was already dead. She would not wake either way.

Helena considered her own possible future. Her return meant the death of the only woman who could help her restore Louis. How could she manage it without Kitty? And yet, here and now, Helena had not yet been born, though this was where Louis lived and was alive. There was no other option.

It seemed no choice at all, but Helena refused to settle. She was burning now. Her bones sang with power and she felt like a finely honed blade, sharp and deadly. She refused to live without Louis. It came to Helena, then, in the midst of the flames.

Aunt Kitty has a past.

Though Helena had seen Kitty dead on the flagstones, Helena knew Kitty had lived to a very old age. She must have woken at some point. Helena glanced over the lake, still dark and calm. The swan fluttered its feathers. *Kitty wakes and then it comes to this, one hundred years later, and then I make the choice and she wakes again. This could have happened a million times over and none would be the wiser.* Helena looked at Ludwig helplessly. *Maybe that is what he meant when he said he'd been here for years. Everyone knows it—the past cannot be changed.*

The king put his finger to his lips as if to silence her. "How did you come to be in this place?"

Helena revealed her suspicions. "I saw myself in a mirror. I fainted and woke up here."

Ludwig gazed at her sadly and said nothing.

"I broke the mirror. Did I somehow enter her memory through it?"

"It would appear to be so."

"What did she do to that mirror?"

"Katza did nothing but have you use it."

Helena did not have to ask why. She remembered the letter. Kitty wanted to change the past and thought she had found a way to do it.

"I think she meant for me to be here."

"No, she never does. Katza only means for you to look into the mirror. You are the vehicle through which she plans her own return. Somehow time stops and you arrive in her stead."

One of us must wake.

It has happened before, Ludwig's words proved it. What happens to Helena? Nothing, she said to herself, until I am born. And then I live for a while, and then I end up here. What kind of life is that?

No. I will have Louis. Aunt Kitty must not wake, nor does she deserve to. Anger at the old woman's manipulations seared her. *The vehicle.* She spat upon the ground. The king coughed. The swan did not move.

The scent of fresh bread came on the wind. It reminded Helena of Hope, rolling out dough. Her mood shifted again.

She missed Hope, she thought with surprise, and the comfort of the kitchen where Hope kept all in order.

That life, Helena realized upon slow reflection, was a motion Helena made, day after day as she walked the halls of house in endless circles. There was no joy in it. As she understood joy, it bunkered down inside her and made itself at home.

Stop, she said to herself. I don't want any more parts. Eight is more than enough. Let me just use the gifts I was made with. The important thing here is Louis. The gifts were individually silent, but their need was somehow united. They all cried for Louis from the deep muscles of Helena's heart.

If Katza wakes in the past, the past will repeat. Louis will die, and he was what Helena wanted. The past has repeated, she reminded herself. How could she possibly change it? A war of desires erupted. Louis' life was what Kitty wanted, but Helena had to accept that in this, their wishes were one.

Helena darted a quick glance at the king. He was patiently waiting while the swan seemed to sleep at his side.

It all came down to Louis; she had to restore him to life. It was what Kitty wanted. It was what Helena wanted. If she had to guess, Helena would say it was what all of the sisters wanted. There must somehow be a way. Helena recalled the sad, dead lump on the flagstones as a slow but thrilling idea began to form.

Katza was dead on the flagstones. In order for everything following to happen, she had to come back to life.

I must have the power. It must be me who restores her.

And, Helena thought with excitement, *if I can do it for her, I can do it for Louis.* Katza could stay dead on the flagstones forever, for all Helena cared. Helena would wake and Louis would live. Helena's face turned red as blood rushed through her body. She grabbed Ludwig by his sleeves and began to dance around him. The swan fluffed out its feathers, startled, and then settled down again on the grass. The king let Helena have her moment. He'd seen it all before.

Into her frenzy a stray thought spun.

Unless Katza wakes now, I have no time to return to.

Her body stopped moving. She stared across the lake as though her answer lay under its waves.

This is why she makes the choice she does, time and time again. The only hope is for Katza to live and finally succeed in her own attempt to save Louis. There was nothing Helena could do but this. Katza must have the chance to keep Louis from dying and for that, Katza must live. Helena sighed and hung her head. Need filled her as the swan fell into her line of vision. Its calm eye gazed into hers blankly, too opaque to read. She doubled over and her knees hit the ground.

Helena must give up her life for Katza's and the chance to save Louis. It was there all along, inside her. The gift of life comes at the cost of life, and debts must always be paid. She might be reborn, she might not—if Katza succeeded, the future would change. Louis would live, but Helena might not again. She suddenly saw how the past has altered the future.

"I've made my choice."

Helena rose to her feet shakily, pulled herself upright with the help of the king.

"It will be Katza who wakes."

Of course he knew. She'd done this countless times already.

"I must say goodbye to the house." She could not bring herself to say, *to my family*, but she had to give her regards to the women who had created her. The power she'd inherited from each of them demanded nothing less.

CHAPTER 35

HELENA ROAMED THE HALLS AIMLESSLY, PEEKED INTO EVERY door and then entered the cold ballroom, where she began to dismiss her followers. She found five of her aunts and returned their gifts to each one. She first went to Thekla's side and straightened her dress. She ran her hand over Thekla's young cheeks, trying to smooth out her pain.

"You should never stop playing the piano," Helena said, "since you love it so very much."

Hilda and Helga were cute as could be as they played quietly in a corner. They sat on the floor, legs crossed, beside a grand old lady who clenched a parasol in her fist. Ringlets of hair fell into their faces as between them they wove a cat's cradle. Helena tucked a string around Helga's finger and kissed small Hilda's cheek. Zilli and Ingeburg shyly clung to their father's legs. Zilli had a star-struck look in her eyes while Ingeburg's hinted at boredom.

It was a strange thing Helena did. Peace was not one of her eight parts and yet it comfortably entered. There wasn't space for much else, she thought, until she saw Eva asleep in her father's arms.

Helena was humbled. Was I ever held like that? She cast

her memory as far back as she could. Yes, I was, by Hope. I will remember next time, Helena said to herself, to thank her. "Sweet dreams," she said to Eva as she put a finger to the child's tiny brow.

Helena's step was surprisingly light as she danced through the wide, quiet room. She said her farewells to the guests and their presents, and to the mirrors that caught her reflection as she twirled by. She left the guests to what dreams they swam in and departed through the back of the room.

The door to the library behind it was open; she had to peek in at the books. There on the shelf for anyone to see was the blue volume that listed the gifts, the book Kitty had held in her hands on the far side of the mirror. Helena pulled it down and opened it; the pages were crisp and clean. So many gifts, she wondered, as she flipped through to the end. If it was the same book she'd seen in the mirror, her aunts' names would be there.

In order of age they were written: Katza, Thekla, Helga and Hilda, Zilli, Ingeburg, Eva, and Elfrieda—the names of the eight sisters who had made her. And there, one hundred years too early, as though written in invisible ink freshly revealed, was Helena's name and gifts noted in order of their reception.

Helena blinked and waited for the letters to rearrange themselves. All of her gifts were accurate except for Eva's. Eva, the book said, had lastly given her sleep.

Not life, as Helena had for so long believed, but sleep. Helena thought of all the mornings her aunts had struggled to wake her, of how easily and deeply she'd always slept, of how tired she was in the evenings and how glad she was, each night, when it was time for bed. She never, not once that she could remember, had a bad night's sleep.

Sleep. So obvious that she'd missed it.

The book slid back into place without concern for her confusion. She understood it now; she believed it. Kitty had given her death and scared them all. That gift, she knew, had been in her all along, as had Eva's. So what had Helena been searching for all of those years? There had been something missing, she *knew* it.

Helena thought back to that silent room, where Thekla stood pointing a rifle at Kitty, with Eva right behind her. Is that what had happened? Had Eva put the whole world to sleep to stop Thekla's finger from pulling the trigger? Everyone but me, Helena thought. I must have slipped through the mirror before sleep had a chance to catch me. Helena frowned. Life was never in her. It was never hers to create.

She would have broken then, but another thought restored her. *I have learned of this a hundred times over.* It did not matter; nothing would matter unless Kitty could change the future. Somehow Kitty must wake.

It must happen, Helena thought. *It has happened before.*

Helena, exhausted and realizing it, looked forward now to the end. She would finish her journey in the place where it had begun.

She went to the room in which she'd left Kitty, what seemed now a long time ago. It was empty and dark, but for what light shone in from the hall.

She was doing the right thing—she must be. She was

doing the only thing she could to give Louis a chance at life and herself an opportunity to have him. All was lost if she returned to the future, and all its attraction was gone. The path ahead was clear and she was ready to follow it, as soon as this last thing was done. The stair was as she remembered it; the little door at the top was unlocked. There was a ledge and on it a candle and matches. She lit the wick and reached for the door. There was no lock, she realized as she grasped the handle and recalled the now useless key.

The room itself was also not quite as she'd left it—the mirror hung intact on the wall. Helena put the candle on the floor and placed her hands on the solid glass. She looked steadily into her own eyes.

"I'm sorry," she said, "but I cannot go back."

CHAPTER 36

"SOMETIMES YOU JUST HAVE TO LET PEOPLE GO."
Hope held the last fragment of mirror in her shaking hand. It seemed such an easy truism. Hope knew otherwise. She turned the small piece of glass in her fingers and was not the first person to marvel at how, sometimes, the fate of all we hold dear rests on such simple things.

She took the pouch from around her neck. Inside was a large, bright spider. Hope untied the cord and laid the pouch on the mirror. The spider crept out and moved quickly across the glass. She watched it chase the light into the window, where it started to weave a web. Hope smiled and looked back at the floor.

The mirror revealed Helena's image on its cracked surface. The lines split her in tiny parts, Hope's glue held her together. Downstairs, Thekla aimed her rifle while Kitty waited for the bullet. The words Kitty had spoken so long ago came back to haunt Hope now. Kitty had been right—the life Helena knew was over, broken beyond real repair. Hope felt it, clenched her fist around it and watched as a drop of blood ran over her palm. Hope had made a promise sixteen years ago. *Whatever happens, I will do my best to mend it.* Hope swallowed the lesson that Kitty had never learned and prepared to face her future. If Helena did change the past, Hope would have none.

Though Hope had never had children, she knew what it meant to mother one. Now she thought she might also know how it feels when that child grows and is finally gone. They would all break because of her gifts, if Helena could not save them. Hope wanted badly to reach in and grab Helena's hand, to pull her back through the mirror and hold her as though she was her own.

How far had Kitty's spell gone? It was very strange magic. How many people get a chance to go back? Not many, as far as Hope knew. Even stranger—how many do and don't even know it?

Hope painted glue on the last piece of glass and fitted it into place with the others. Helena's face gazed back at her, complete. Their eyes locked. There was no way for Hope to know how much time she would have or if she could even force her voice through the doorway. She must use the moment wisely.

Hope sat in a circle of light on a hard chair in a secret room. She was dirty and tired and sore, but she was content. She'd kept her promise; the rest was now up to fate. Hope glanced at the spider, still in the window. There was no guarantee it would do any more than spin out a spider's web, but such is the nature of chance and Hope knew it. She bent her knees to the cold wood of the floor and breathed onto the glass. After so much effort, this was a simple thing, too.

"Break the spell," she called out to Helena.

"Break the mirror!"

Hope's syllables fell into the cracks in the glass, where they mingled with the mercury on its back and crossed through to the other side. Hope put everything she was into those words: nursemaid, housekeeper, cook, and mother. She smiled. Though Helena's reflection did not answer, Hope knew she had been heard.

℘ ☙

In the mirror, Helena watched as her face transformed and became that of an old, frightful hag. Her mouth moved of its own volition. Helena leaned forward to hear the words. The old crone smiled and suddenly Helena knew her. The force of Hope's love drew Helena's face to the mirror, where their breath mingled on the surface of the glass. She heard Hope clearly and drank down every word.

Hope had been there since the beginning, as constant as the sun crossing over the lake each morning. Though kinship was not in her making, Helena felt it arrange itself inside of her. As Helena watched, Hope's face began to fade.

"Don't go," she sobbed at the mirror, but only her own features responded to her plea.

On the other side of the glass, where Helena could not see her, Hope rose wearily from the floor and brushed off the front of her dress. Though her old bones protested, she brought her foot down in the center of the mirror. Helena's eight parts shattered with the glass.

Helena stood in front of the mirror, eyes wide and face flushed. She was a tree whose bark was stripped by the wind, a rose whose petals had suddenly fallen. Helena clung to the mirror as she was turned inside out. Katza will wake, Helena thought, and the past will remain unchanged, because the past never changes. It is me—I keep us all in this circle with my decision. I will never have Louis, no matter what choice I make. The last piece of her shattered and hit the ground.

Break the spell, Hope had said. Hope *knew,* she thought, amazed that Hope had been able to find her. Then, *Hope is alive and still awake in the future.* If Aunt Kitty wakes now, Hope, too, will cease to exist.

The entire future must begin anew.

Hope was right, it was a spell, but both Helena and Kitty had cast it. Kitty's spell had brought them to this, but it was Helena's decision that led them back to it time after time. The children in the ballroom stood no chance; the future would only repeat and swing back in upon them without them ever knowing it had happened before. They must be very tired, Helena thought. Like me. She owed all of them, and Hope, so very much.

Break the mirror, Hope had said. The house was still and silent around her. Helena, weightless, took a deep breath and touched the raw core at her center, where her inheritance sat, exposed. She knew now the name of her power, should have guessed it all along. She was no different from the rest of the family—she had the power to give gifts, too. This is how she wakes Kitty, again and again.

The power to give and the power to take away—the two are inseparable. Time, Helena decided, is too dangerous a gift; it lets you see too much. It is fine, Helena thought, to be stuck in the past, as long as you eventually get out of it. She ran her finger over the edge of the mirror, drew it around the circumference and back to where she began. Helena could do nothing about Kitty's gift of time, but this possible future could finally be sealed off forever.

She stepped away from the mirror and unclasped the chains around her neck. The locket gleamed, but the key was dull and hung listlessly from her fingers. Such a small thing, she thought, to unlock such complicated doors. She clenched her hand around them both and drew back her arm. There is one door this key will not open, ever again. Helena closed her eyes and released her power.

The past met the future as the glass exploded. Helena instinctively covered her face as the mirror shattered. Shards shot into the walls and around her head like arrows. The sound was deafening. Helena wrapped her arms around her head as the last pieces fell to the floor in a hailstorm of tiny daggers. Mirrored fragments of glass littered the room. Candlelight streamed out through the sliver of window, a remnant of a future in which it had been pried it open. A spider vanished into the frame as Helena watched. She pulled a stray piece of mirror out of her hair and looked into it. All she saw was her own eye gazing back. She dropped the glass and slid to the floor, unconscious.

CHAPTER 37

IN THE HOUSE, CANDLES BEGAN TO FLICKER. THE GUESTS started to breathe and to slowly regain their motion as time, that heaving behemoth, began to turn.

Outside, the storm raged. Rain slashed across Louis' face and his horse almost spun out of control. Suddenly, from high in the house, a flash of light shone in a window Louis was certain had never been there. It drew his attention back to the courtyard. He saw a body crumpled on the flagstones behind him. Louis reined in the horse and leapt from its back, ducking through the leaves and limbs pelting him as he ran to the sodden girl's side.

My god, Louis thought, *my sister.* The king's message forgotten, he carefully lifted her from the ground and carried her through the storm. Cook heard him kick open the door to the kitchen and sent a girl out to find Magdalena.

"What has happened?" Magdalena shouted as she hurried through the kitchen, her fine dress spotting with ash and oil. She saw Louis holding Katza and stopped with a hand to her mouth. Cook chased the maids out as Magdalena fought for composure.

"Take her to her room. I'll have Papa summon the

doctor." Magdalena could not say it, but Louis saw it in her eyes.

"She is breathing," he said.

"Take her. I'll be right there."

Magdalena lifted her skirts and ran from the room with no thought for dignity. Louis shifted his sister's weight in his arms. He felt young again, though he never had a chance to grow old. He wondered, briefly, what the king was doing, but Katza's weight in his arms meant far more.

Louis carried her to her room and laid her on the cold bed. The shutters were pulled tight against the windows. He lit the lamp by her bedside and tucked a blanket around her still form. Together they waited as below, the guests bid the family goodnight.

The doctor arrived two hours later. His diagnosis: a coma. Keep her comfortable, he said, there was nothing more they could do. The Baroness looked in once the guests were gone, but only shook her head in sorrow. She had her own worries to tend.

Katza looked peaceful, as though she were sleeping, as they all should have been at that hour. Louis insisted that their parents go to their rest and let him watch over his sister. They fussed, but agreed and left him. Though the night was long, Louis did not falter. He did not once think of the king. He sat on the edge of the bed beside Katza and moved only when the first tendrils of light began to crawl over the lake. Dawn brought with it the heavy scent of roses. Louis stretched and went to the window. The rain had stopped in the night, the earth was washed clean and around the house, every rose on its stem was in bloom.

Katza seemed to be resting comfortably. It wouldn't hurt to leave for a moment, he thought. She would like a bouquet of flowers. He slipped out the door and went into the gardens, where lush roses of the deepest red waved in the cool morning breeze. He cut a handful and put the bunch to his face, drew in the perfume and let it cover his hair. They reminded him of Katza.

In Katza's room he arranged all but one in a porcelain vase on the table near the bed. The last rose he kept for his sister. Her head was turned into the pillow and her breath disturbed a strand of hair that lay on her cheek. She is beautiful, Louis said to himself as he sat gently on the mattress. Her hair was the color of golden wheat and her neck was as slender as willow. He let his fingers run along Katza's jaw and brushed the rose across her brow. Louis was drawn to his sister's smooth, red lips. He leaned in and placed a gentle kiss on her mouth.

Katza stirred beside him; he sat up and watched in disbelief as her eyes slowly opened. They did not focus on him.

"Is it you, Louis? You have been so long in coming. I feel as though I've been sleeping for at least a hundred years." Her voice was faint, as though it came from a place far away.

Louis wrapped his arms around and held her as close as he dared. "I am here, Katza. All is well."

"Louis? I can't see you. Why can't I see you?" Katza clung to him, and trembled.

Louis took her hand in one of his and waved the other in front of her eyes. "Do you see my hand, Katza? Do you see anything at all?"

Katza felt for his lapels and drew him close to her face, ran her fingers over his nose and tangled them in his hair.

"No," she said, "I see nothing. Louis, I think I am blind."

৪০ ৫৪

"This is very strange. Very strange."

The doctor shook his head, for he'd never seen anything like it and he'd certainly seen some inexplicable things in this family. He removed his spectacles, wiped the lenses with a handkerchief and put them in his pocket, deliberately, as though attempting to buy time.

"What is it?" Magdalena was impatient to know why her daughter was blind again.

The doctor cleared his throat, an awful guffawing sound that caused Katza, who could not see it coming, to jump in her bed. "It appears to me that a sliver of glass is embedded in each of her pupils."

"What?" said Magdalena.

"How is that possible?" asked Louis.

"You say you found her on the flagstones. There must have been broken glass on the ground where she fell." He didn't seem to believe his own words, but he stood by them. "Unusual, but perfectly reasonable."

Magdalena looked as though she wanted to throttle him. Papa just shook his head, sadly, as though he could not believe his ears.

"Reasonable?" Papa said. "Is that what they call it?"

The doctor coughed into his hand.

"Is she in pain?" Louis had to know.

The doctor turned to Louis and scratched his chin in thought. "She doesn't seem to be. If she mentions any discomfort, please let me know."

Katza, who ignored the doctor once he was done poking his fingers into her eyes, finally spoke. "I am fine. Please leave. I want to be alone with my brother."

The doctor seemed eager to do as Katza requested and he and Papa went to settle the fee. Mama swept a hand across Katza's brow and then left them.

Katza held out her hand and Louis took it.

"Louis? What happened to me?" The night was a blur; the last thing she remembered was chasing him into the rain. "I had such terrible dreams."

Louis swallowed his guilt. "You followed me into the courtyard. You must have slipped and hit your head. The doctor came in the night and said you were in a coma. We did not expect you to wake."

"I didn't either. I didn't think it would ever end."

He drew her in. "It is over now. I am here."

"I'm so hungry. Will you help me down the stairs?" Katza's stomach growled and Louis laughed.

"Of course."

Katza wrapped her arm in Louis' and let him lead the way. He was cautious, but Katza's feet recalled each step and her hand lingered lightly on the banister, as though her body remembered what it was to be blind. When they reached the first floor, Katza stopped. Some part of her dream still lingered. She pressed her hand into Louis' arm.

"Do you remember the secret room we found when we were young? It had a mirror on the wall. Is it still there?"

"I have no idea. I haven't been there in years."

"Take me."

Why blind Katza would care now about the mirror Louis did not know, but he humored her despite his misgivings. The stairway was narrow and dark, but that wouldn't matter to Katza. He took a candle for himself and guided her to the room, where he opened the door onto a disaster.

The mirror was in pieces on the floor.

"It is broken," he said as he kicked a shard with his toe. "And the window has been uncovered. Very strange."

Katza's face creased in confusion. She was sure she needed that mirror for something, but now it was gone.

"Wait," Louis said as he bent to the floor. "I've found a key."

He pressed the cold metal into Katza's hand; she brought it to her face and touched her cheek with the metal. "I wonder what it opens," she said, and then dropped it as Louis folded her hand into his.

They closed the door behind them. The sound of Papa rattling his newspaper drew them to the table. They were late; the others were already gathered together for breakfast. The house glowed as morning light filled the windows. Mama pulled out a chair for Katza to sit in and Louis guided her to it. As they reached her seat, an attendant rushed in and handed Papa a letter.

"My god," Papa suddenly shouted.

Mama, Louis and Thekla turned towards him as the other

children giggled on in their corner, unconcerned by the look on his face. Katza's hand tightened on Louis' arm.

"What is it?" Mama asked.

"The king," Papa cried. "Ludwig was found in the lake last night. They say it might have been murder!"

CHAPTER 38

HELENA WOKE. SHE WAS TIRED, HER SINEWS PINCHED AND burned and her neck cracked as she turned it. She was wearing the same dress, but it was faded and brittle, as though it had been abandoned in some musty closet more than a century ago. It was daybreak and the soft grass of the grounds glistened with dew. She was on the wide, stone steps at the front of the house. She did not recall leaving the hidden room, but was still well aware of what she had done there.

Given two choices, it seemed she had made a third. Had it happened this way before? Life erupted around her as the sun rose above the horizon. Birds began to call out to each other, both in the trees and over the lake, and at her feet insects roamed the cold stone of the steps. Around her, life was restored to its usual pattern and flow of minutes and hours. The nightmare was over. Helena frowned. She was not supposed to wake.

She raised her hand to rub at her eyes and stood, motionless with incomprehension, as her fingers came into sight. Gone was the silken skin of youth with which she was so familiar. In its place was a gnarled talon, somehow attached to an equally wrinkled and limpid arm that she knew, without a doubt, grew from her own shoulder. She willed the hand to movement, pulled a tendril of hair from behind her and blinked when she saw, instead of dark tresses, a skein of cobweb pinched in her fingers.

She was old and felt age with a suddenness that brought her to her knees. She knew a brief moment of insane humor when she realized that she might not be able to rise. She reached out toward the briars beside her. Surely they would lend an old woman their assistance. They did, and as she wrapped her hand around the thick vines and pulled herself to her feet, Helena felt she knew what it was to be ancient.

The lives of her aunts and their mother and her mother before her coursed through her veins as she clung painfully to the roses. Their memories seeped out of the foundation stones like water, up through the briars and into Helena as thorns pricked her hands and petals fell into her hair. All of their lives took root in her and blossomed.

She reeled from the flood. Her old pores opened and drank it in but her mind, still caught in the spaces of youth and inexperience, could not grasp it all at once. She steadied herself and tried to organize the swirling images of so many lives into some kind of coherent story.

Every detail was there, a parade of knowledge that settled and shifted until Helena thought she would burst. Her gifts would have loved it, but they were gone. Her heart thudded, her breath rasped in her chest and her back ached as though it was on fire, but she could not stop the flow of time. She opened herself and let all of them in, held them and cherished each one. When all of the past settled in her, a wave of the future arrived. The memories Katza had stored flew like birds into Helena's hair and scattered the happy succession of time. They shouldn't be there, that future was gone, but they were and they needed a home. Helena took them in as well until she was full, and then she let all but one of them go.

Louis. She knew now why the sight of him had caused her so much turmoil. It had been Katza's longing and Katza's spell and had nothing to do with Helena. Yet Louis was now part of her, too. His memory she would take with her, wherever her path led now.

Helena placed one foot before the other and slowly made her way down the steps, left the roses to bow at the sun and the household to go on as it would without her. None of them could remember her now. The lake at the edge of the grounds, the swing by the shore and Ludwig, lost king of a magical land: these things beckoned. It would be good to rest her bones by the water, if only the seat was not too hard.

Ludwig waited by the shore. The swan watched Helena approach as the small boat rocked on the waves. The king's eyes narrowed as she approached. She was not as he remembered.

"What have you done?"

"The same thing I always do. I chose Katza."

"Something has changed."

Her gifts were gone and with them her hunger. Helena was glad to find she did not need an answer. She brushed what felt like a spider from the back of her neck and smirked. "Has it?"

The king laughed up at the clear sky. "You must know, Helena, how you have finally freed us."

Helena shrugged.

"Hope told me what to do."

$$\text{\small ✤❧}$$

The family was speechless. None could imagine a world without Ludwig, their mad, dreaming king. All faces turned to Louis, even Katza's, who didn't care that she could not see him.

Louis' eyes closed. He thought he heard church bells in the far distance; his ears rang, his head spun and he felt a great weight rise up, as though it had wings, and leave him. Katza put her arms around his waist and clung there. The king's letter had turned to pulp in his pocket, the rain had soaked through and the ink had bled into his coat. *Ludwig is gone*, a voice said in the dark, *but you still have your sister. Do not fail her again.*

Louis opened his eyes and saw his family around him.

"Louis?" Katza said in a whisper.

"I'm right here."

$$\text{\small ✤❧}$$

The swan rose to its feet and stretched out its wide, bright wings. Sparks caught on the tips of its feathers and spread until the bird was engulfed in flame. Helena and the king watched in fascination as from the swan's fallen feathers, Louis rose.

Helena blinked in the morning light. Louis' curls were dark and thick, his coat was a deep red and his black boots gleamed in the sun. He was beautiful, but she had no reaction. It was just good to see him alive.

"Katza kept him, too, trapped in memory like the roses, but now that memory is gone." Ludwig turned to Helena as Louis smiled and faded into light.

She watched as the king reached under his cloak and pulled out a magnificent crown. Fine and thin, it was spun out of silver sheer as cobwebs and woven in the shape of a swan. Diamonds glittered at the center of tiny spirals whorled by a careful hand, and a wing curved gracefully outward on either side. He held it out to Helena, who pushed it away.

"Please, I don't want another gift." She looked at her ragged dress and wrinkled elbows. "It's too beautiful for me anyway."

To her surprise Ludwig, the king, leaned in and kissed her.

"No, Helena. The thorns concealing your beauty have parted. This is your inheritance."

She closed her eyes as its weight settled on her brow.

"Now is it done?" she asked when he stepped away.

"It is done," he replied, "and time."

She squinted her eyes at the king. "May I ask you one question before we go?"

The king nodded. "Yes, of course you may."

"The stories are incomplete. How did you die?" Helena was curious, no more.

"Does it matter now? Last night is a fading dream." Ludwig's lips curved in the tiniest smile. "Tell the storytellers I am not dead, only sleeping."

"You are mad," she said.

"So they say," the king replied.

Ludwig took Helena's withered hand and helped her onto the vessel that waited by the shore. The black forest bowed as the swan-shaped boat sailed into the distance, as though drawn by a calm west wind. The lake was smooth as glass. Light breached the clouds; their reflection appeared on the water.

It lingered long after they'd gone.

About the Author

Erzebet YellowBoy is an author, bookbinder and editor whose work has appeared in *Fantasy Magazine, Electric Velocipede, Behind the Wainscot, Running with the Pack, Haunted Legend*s, and more. She is the founder of Papaveria Press, a micropress specialising in fairy tales and fantasies, and is the fiction editor of *Cabinet des Fées*, an online journal of fairy tales. Visit her website at www.erzebet.com.